ROUGH CIDER

ROUGH CIDER

Peter Lovesey

G.K. Hall & Co. • Chivers Press
Waterville, Maine USA Bath, England

This Large Print edition is published by G.K. Hall & Co., USA
and by Chivers Press, England.

Published in 2002 in the U.S. by arrangement with
Soho Press, Inc.

Published in 2002 in the U.K. by arrangement with
the author.

U.S. Hardcover 0-7838-9772-3 (Core Series)
U.K. Hardcover 0-7540-4853-5 (Chivers Large Print)
U.K. Softcover 0-7540-4854-3 (Camden Large Print)

The text of this Large Print edition is unabridged.
Other aspects of the book may vary from the original edition.

Set in 16 pt. Plantin by Christina S. Huff.

Printed in the United States on permanent paper.

British Library Cataloguing-in-Publication Data available

Library of Congress Cataloging-in-Publication Data

Lovesey, Peter.
    Rough cider / Peter Lovesey.
    p. cm.
    ISBN 0-7838-9772-3 (lg. print : hc : alk. paper)
    1. World War, 1939–1945 — England — Fiction.   2. Executions
and executioners — Fiction.   3. Fathers and daughters —
Fiction.   4. Americans — England — Fiction.   5. Somerset
(England) — Fiction.   6. Large type books.   I. Title.
PR6062.O86 R6 2002
    823´.914—dc21   2001051772

Rough Cider

ONE

When I was nine, I fell in love with a girl of twenty named Barbara, who killed herself.

True.

It's an extraordinary story. I've been telling myself for years that I must put it in writing. I can't expect the memories to stay vivid forever. I'm past fifty now.

I have any number of excuses for delaying so long. Where should I start, for instance? Not in 1943, for sure.

To tell it right, I must take you into a self-service restaurant in Reading in 1964, where you meet me at the self-assured age of twenty-nine, eating sausages and chips and rashly trying to read Machiavelli's *The Prince* at the same time. A Friday lunch. I know it was Friday because at the end of the week I was in the habit of escaping from the university for a quiet couple of hours on my own. My luckless duty as the most underemployed member of staff in the history department was to offer a course on Europe in the twentieth century to all-comers in the first year. Like many other fiascos, my course was the brainchild of a committee, this one dedicated to promoting a concept known as supportive studies. It was optional and would not be examined. The "all-comers" consisted of a phalanx of political agitators who filled the two front rows, plus sundry casual callers who came in to sleep because all seats were taken in the library. After it I was in no mood for luncheon and pretentious conversation in the senior refectory.

"Excuse me, is this place taken?"

I raised my eyes from the book and stared. It's a long cultural leap from Machiavelli to a girl with pouting lips like Bardot's, blond hair, and gold-rimmed glasses.

She was carrying a full tray.

I took a glance around me. There was no reason for her to have come to my table. The restaurant was three-quarters empty. There were two unoccupied tables to my right.

I'd better explain that I'm obliged to use a stick to get about. My right leg is practically useless. At thirteen I became a victim of polio. Ninety-nine people in a hundred who contract the virus display only minor and temporary symptoms. I was the hundredth. Compared with others I've met, mine is a small disability. I try not to let it limit my possibilities. I refuse to wear a leg-iron, so I keep myself vertical with a stick, an ostentatious ebony cane with an inlaid silver band and a leather handle. The reason I mention this is that from time to time I'm bothered by well-meaning people who impose themselves on me to attest their concern for the disabled. My first thought when I saw the girl with the tray was that she was one of these. I didn't want to be patronized, even by a stunningly good-looking girl.

I guessed from her age (she was not more than twenty) and the glasses that she was a student, but her clothes were definitely more town than gown; red chiffon scarf, black blouse, and peacock-blue corduroy skirt with dark stockings and black, sling-back shoes. Something was wrong, though. Even to my inexpert eye the skirt was inches too long for Britain in 1964. Her accent was unfamiliar, also, which may have explained why she didn't understand the form in a British self-service restaurant.

I gave her the benefit of the doubt and cleared my newspaper from the place opposite.

She sat down, reaching behind her neck to pull a thick, blond plait over her right shoulder.

"Thank you. I'm really obliged to you."

So she was American.

The balance shifted back in favor of the university: very likely she was one of the new intakes who wasn't yet into more casual clothes. She even might have been so raw as to have sat through the lecture I had just delivered.

"Hope you don't object to the smell of curry," the girl said with a nervous laugh as she lifted the metal cover off her plate. "If there's anything hot and spicy on the menu, I'm enslaved. Mexican food is my number-one favorite, but

9

you can't get it here. Have you eaten Mexican? You should. You really should."

So she wanted conversation, as well as a place at my table. I was sure I recognized the zealous tone of the do-gooder. I pretended to discover an interest in a wrestling-bill on the wall beside me. A barrel-shaped brute called Angel Harper was scheduled to grapple in the Town Hall with Shaggy Sterne, who was the hairiest human I'd ever seen.

"You're from the university, am I right?" she said, as if an interest in professional wrestling were positive proof. Then, not waiting for an answer, "Would you care for some water? I swear I shall die if I don't have water with this."

She sprang up like a fireman and went to look for water.

I shifted my eyes to her retreating figure. The white ribbon at the top of the blond plait danced to the swing of her hips. Let's admit it — deep down I was flattered that she'd chosen to join me.

She came back with two glasses of water and placed them on the table. She had pale, slender hands and clear varnish on her nails. "I wasn't sure if you said you wanted any, but if you don't, I guess there's a fair chance I shall be able to use a second glass."

I moved my lips in a token response and looked down at my book.

A few seconds passed before she took a sip of water and started again. "Forgive me if I'm wrong, but aren't you Theo Sinclair?"

I shut the book and frowned. She'd used my name. My *first* name. This was 1964, remember, when we addressed undergraduates, even freshers straight from school, as Mr. or Miss, unless we were playing rugby with them or recruiting for the Communist Party. We gave respect and expected it in return.

As before, when she'd asked a direct question, she was too nervous or too loquacious to let it stand. "I'm Alice Ashenfelter from Waterbury, Connecticut. Do you know the States? Waterbury is a couple hours' bus ride from New York City. You don't mind if we talk? I heard so much about English people being reserved and everything, but I found it isn't true at all when you get over the first bit. Aren't you going to ask me how I got to know your name?"

I answered, "As it happens, no." As I mentioned, I'm not proud of the way I reacted. I've tried since to analyze my coolness towards her. I suppose in a perverse way I resented the fact that an extremely attractive young woman felt safe enough with me to make the sort of approach she had.

I'd got through my main course. Generally I finished with a coffee, but I decided to miss it. I looked at my watch, wiped my mouth, said in a measured voice, "Time I was moving on," gathered my book and newspaper, reached for my stick, got up, and moved away.

Foolishly, I thought I wouldn't be bothered

11

again by Alice Ashenfelter.

At two, when I returned to my office in the Faculty of Arts building, she was waiting in there, standing in front of the Paul Klee print beside the filing cabinet.

"Hi."

I turned right about and went to see Carol Dangerfield, the department secretary. Cool Carol of the beehive hairstyle, the only member of the admin staff who always survived enrollment week without a migraine or a bust-up with the prof. She kept us sane.

"That girl in my office — the American — did you tell her to wait in there?"

"Why, yes, Dr. Sinclair. Did I do wrong?"

"What did she say she wanted?"

"I don't know that she mentioned anything. She simply asked to see you. I thought she must be one of your tutor group, so I sent her in to wait."

"Her name is Ashenfelter. Is she one of ours?"

Carol Dangerfield frowned. "Unless she's a fresher . . ." She opened the card index on her desk. "Apparently not. Perhaps she's one of Professor Byron's intakes. I could check with his secretary."

"Doesn't matter," I said. "I'll ask the girl herself."

But when I returned to my office, Alice Ashenfelter was no longer there.

I dismissed her from my mind. I had a host of things to do before the end of the afternoon. Everything that could be put off during the week got left for those two precious hours at the end of Friday: letters, phone calls, requisitions, a couple of tutorials, circulars to initial from the dean and the prof, and a visit to the library to equip myself for next week's lectures.

This session would be my fifth at Reading University, and although I'd never considered myself an academic, having scraped an upper second at Southampton where I was better known as a bridge player than as an historian, there had never been much prospect of anything else. A specialized knowledge of Europe in the Middle Ages didn't open many doors in 1956. It turned out that the friendly professor at Bristol who offered me a research scholarship was interested mainly in the renaissance of the Senior Common Room bridge club. But with it came some lecturing experience and ultimately the Ph.D. and the move to Reading. There, I made strenuous efforts to fit the image of the thrusting young lecturer. I shaved off my beard, abandoned bridge in favor of snooker, bought a red MG and had it adapted for me to drive, and took a lease on a house by the river at Pangbourne. All in all, life was treating me well — which is when you want to look out.

Towards four I was starting to fill my briefcase when Carol Dangerfield put her head around the door. "Have you got a minute? I thought you might be interested. I've been doing some checking. You said the girl in your office was named Ashenfelter?"

"Alice Ashenfelter."

"Well, she's not one of ours. There's no student of that name registered in the university."

"Is that so?" I said. "I wonder what she was doing in here, then."

"She didn't leave a note on your desk or anything?"

"No." I shifted my papers to check. "There's nothing here."

"Funny."

"What's funny?"

"Well, I mentioned her to Sally Beach, who runs the bookshop and knows just about everything that goes on in this place, and she said an American girl like that — blond, with glasses and a pigtail — was hanging around the union bar last night asking if anyone knew you."

I frowned. "Asking for me by name?"

She nodded and gave a quick smile. "You've got a secret admirer, Dr. Sinclair."

"Come off it, Carol. I've never clapped eyes on the girl before today. She happened to sit at my table in Ernestine's this lunchtime."

"Happened to?"

I fingered the knot of my tie, remembering how it had happened.

"She had a chance to talk to you, then," said Carol. "Didn't she say anything?"

"Her name, the town she came from, nothing else of consequence. I didn't exactly encourage

14

her. I mean, what does she want with me, a total stranger?"

"Perhaps she met you somewhere else, on holiday, for instance, and you've forgotten."

"I wouldn't forget. She's, em, unusual. No, I swear I haven't met her. Well, whatever she wanted, I seem to have frightened her off."

"Don't be so sure, Dr. Sinclair," said Carol, staring out of the window. "It's getting dark, I know, but isn't that her down in the car park standing beside your MG?"

TWO

I went down to the Senior Common Room to make myself a coffee. The place was deserted except for a couple of cleaning women who had Sinatra's latest at full volume on the record player in competition with their vacuums. Strictly, they shouldn't have been in there until five, but they were obviously used to having the place to themselves after four on Fridays. Like everyone else, they didn't care to hang about at the end of the week. Everyone except me, apparently. They looked at me as if I were an agent of the head caretaker, but I gestured to them to carry on.

Carol Dangerfield would be at the window of her office, waiting to see the next scene played in the staff car park. Would I invite my blond pursuer into my car and drive into the night with her, or would I hold her at bay with my stick? Well, Carol was in for a disappointment unless she was planning some overtime. I made the coffee, drank it slowly, and practiced snooker shots until well after five.

When I eventually walked out to the car park, it was deserted except for three cars and one girl, reclining against mine. There was a light drizzle on the wind, and you could feel the chill of an October evening. Whiteknights Park is pretty exposed. Alice Ashenfelter was wearing a coat, but she had to be persistent or dedicated or just mad to have stood there so long.

The possibility that she was mad hadn't occurred to me before. There was a girl living next door to us once who developed a passion for our Conservative Member of Parliament. I mean, a real infatuation. It didn't matter that he was happily married with three young children. She used to write him passionate letters at the House of Commons. He staunchly ignored them until she started sending them in larger envelopes with pairs of Marks and Spencer panties. Apparently people in public life are subjected to more of that kind of thing than most of us hear about. Anyway, this girl was schizoid. She ended up breaking into the MP's house at night and getting put away for a few months. The last I heard, she was under permanent sedation.

I nodded to Alice Ashenfelter as if she were just the latest blonde who happened to be leaning against the bonnet of my car on a Friday evening.

She took a step away from the car, clasped her hands in front of her as if in supplication, and said, "Dr. Sinclair, I'm sorry if I embarrassed you, going up to your room like that."

"It didn't embarrass me," I said. "Forget it."

"I wouldn't want to be a nuisance to you."

17

"You're not," I answered with more hope than conviction. "But it's kind of you to mention it. Good night, miss, er . . ."

"Where are you going now?"

"Where I generally go at the end of the day: home." I had the keys out and was fumbling for the door, always an awkward procedure for me.

"Could we talk?"

"Here?" I made it sound like a straight no. I unlocked the door and pulled it open.

"Someplace else. Anyplace you want."

"I don't think so." I dropped my bag and stick into the car and lowered myself onto the seat. The moment I let it take my weight, I knew that I was in trouble.

Alice Ashenfelter said innocently, "It looks like you have a flat tire."

I can cope with most of the functions necessary to maintain a car. I can change a tire. The only thing is that it involves more effort and more groveling on the ground than it would for a man with two good legs. On a damp surface in my gray worsted suit, it was a prospect that I think justified the mild obscenity I uttered.

The girl said, "I'll fix it. Where do you keep your tools?"

I considered the offer. I had a pretty strong suspicion that she'd let down the tire. To accept her help would put me under some kind of obligation. Yet try to get a garage to send out a man on a Friday in the rush hour and see how long you have to wait.

I hauled myself upright and unlocked the boot, intending to do the job myself, but her two hands were quicker than my one at lifting out the jack. She didn't need any help in assembling it, either.

"I can manage without your help," I said.

"It's too damn cold for that kind of he-man crap," said she. "Would you hand me the wrench, please?"

I found myself smiling, and that was fatal. I succumbed to the logic of what she had said. She quickly and competently got on with the job. While she was jacking up the car I unfixed the spare and later I fastened the flat in its place, so I didn't feel totally redundant.

Before she'd finished, I knew I had to offer her a lift at the least. I was prepared to bet she'd let the tire down in the first place, but after her Good Samaritan act, I couldn't drive off and leave her standing in the rain in the deserted car park.

I offered to take her to a pub where she could wash her hands. She got in and we drove to one on the London Road where I was pretty sure we wouldn't meet anyone from the university. When she came out of the ladies', I bought her a lager and lime.

"Now, would you like to tell me what that was about?" I asked.

"Couldn't we just pass a little time getting to know each other?"

"Is that important?"

She stared at me earnestly through her gold frames. "It's normal, isn't it?"

"All right. Tell me what you're doing in England."

"Vacationing."

"In October?"

"A late vacation."

"Catching up on the history or just the history lecturers?"

She reddened and looked into her drink. "That isn't fair and I resent it."

"You mean, there's something special about me?"

She didn't answer. She was fingering the end of her plait like a small, sulky girl. Her hair was parted in a perfectly straight line down the center of her bowed head. She was a true blonde.

"Maybe I imagined that you were pursuing me," I suggested. "Is it the onset of paranoia, do you think?"

She answered in a low voice, "I think you're making this hellishly difficult for me."

"If I knew what it was, I might be able to help. If you're in some kind of trouble, I can probably put you in touch with people who will help you."

She looked away and said petulantly, "Give me a break, will you?"

So we lapsed into silence for an interval.

Finally I made signs of moving and said, "Where are you staying? Can I give you a lift?"

She shook her head. "There's no need. I know where I am now. It's no distance from here."

"I'll be away, then. Thanks for your work on the tire."

She moved her hand a short way across the table, as if to detain me, then thought better of it and curled it around her glass. "I'll come here at lunchtime tomorrow. Could we try again?"

I stared at her, mystified. "Why? What's the point? What are we supposed to try for?"

She bit her lip and said, "You scare me."

I didn't know what response to give. Clearly it wasn't meant as a joke. I shook my head to show that I was at a loss and got up.

"Lunchtime tomorrow," she repeated. "Please, Theo."

THREE

You know the impression Alice Ashenfelter made on me, so I'm not going to explain why I didn't meet her at the pub in Reading on Saturday morning. It must have got through to you by now that I'm not your obliging English gentleman. I just eat like a gentleman. I drove into Pangbourne and did my Saturday shopping at the grocer's (we still had one), half a cooked gammon, some duck pâté, a dozen new-laid eggs, and a fresh melon. Mindful of Saturday night, I picked up a bottle of champagne from the off-license and waited at the garage while my flat tire was inspected. As I had anticipated, they didn't find a puncture. They suggested that there might be a fault in the valve, and I undertook to check the pressure in a day or two. I forgot all about it after that.

The rugby international on the BBC's *Grandstand* occupied me agreeably for most of the afternoon. That evening I took my current girlfriend, Val Paxton, a staff nurse at Reading General, to the Odeon to see *A Hard Day's Night*. Neither of us enjoyed it much. The best I can say is that the facile story line was made bearable by some memorable songs and witty dialogue. Val, who wasn't crazy about the Beatles, would have opted for Losey's *King and Country* at the ABC movie theater, but I didn't want to spend my evening at a court-martial. If you think that's a deplorable attitude for a history lecturer to take to one of the most powerful dramas ever made of the first world war, you're dead right, chum. You're right and I'm honest, okay?

Afterwards, over a drink, Val told me she'd been thinking about our relationship, and we didn't have much going outside the bedroom. Plain speaking: that's what you get from a nurse. She said her time off-duty was too precious to fritter on things she didn't enjoy. She'd been thinking all through the film that something was badly wrong if we both sat there bored for a couple of hours. I asked her what she'd rather have been doing and she said dancing. A great suggestion to make to a guy with a stick.

After that I passed a few comments on the nursing profession and their priorities, and we were soon trading insults. It got worse. This wasn't one of those evenings when a stand-up row ends in a passionate reconciliation. It ended with a curt good night at the gate of the nurses' residence.

It was some time after eleven-thirty when I put the car away and came around the front of the house. When I mentioned earlier that I live by the river at Pangbourne, you probably made the reasonable assumption that I meant the Thames. Anyone hearing of the River Pang would probably place it in China or Burma, but believe me, it has its source in the Wessex Downs and takes a gentle U-shaped course through rural Berkshire for twelve miles or so before joining the Thames from the south at Pangbourne. The Pang is the river that runs past the end of my garden. "River" is perhaps an exaggeration; in reality it's more of an ancient trout stream. The point of telling you this is that my location is more remote than you might have imagined. I'm not isolated, mind — there are three houses within shouting distance — but we don't see many strangers. Which is why I was surprised when my stick touched an obstruction on the garden path that turned out to be a rucksack.

I might easily have fallen over the thing. She'd left it against the mud scraper that I keep by my front door. You'll have gathered that I was not in much doubt about the ownership. Even by moonlight I could see a handkerchief-size Stars and Stripes stitched to the flap. Yet Alice Ashenfelter wasn't in sight.

With my Saturday night already in ruins, I wasn't feeling well disposed towards the fair sex. I took a long breath, found my key, and let myself in without bothering to check whether she was somewhere in the garden. Didn't look round or call out. Closed the door behind me, went into the kitchen, and put on the kettle for my coffee.

I didn't expect her to go away. If for some reason she hadn't seen me come in, she'd certainly notice the lights go on. She'd knock at the door any second, and I'd have to be mentally tough to ignore her. The trouble was that I'm easy prey to her sort of tactics. I knew that if I didn't respond, I'd spend the rest of the night wondering how she'd cope in the open on a Saturday night in my remote corner of Berkshire.

My imagination turned morbid. I pictured myself in the Coroner's Court at Reading trying to explain why I'd callously closed my door on a young visitor to England who was known to me, had helped me change a wheel only the evening before, and had asked nothing more from me than a civil conversation; who, in consequence of my inhospitality, had taken to the road, hitched a lift with a vanload of drunken pop musicians, been sexually abused, and then thrown from the moving vehicle, fatally fracturing her skull. I could even see her parents, over from Waterbury, Connecticut, for the funeral, red-eyed with grief, staring at me across the grave, unable to understand how any fellow human could be so stony-hearted.

To break this unproductive chain of thought, I switched on the television and got a bishop giving the epilogue. It was so timely that I laughed out loud. For God's sake (as the bishop had just remarked), just when I'd been given the elbow by one girl, another was at my door. What was I bellyaching about?

I turned off the bishop, took a sip of coffee, and considered the options. Already it was midnight. If Alice Ashenfelter had come on a visit, she was planning to stay the night. You've heard of the swinging sixties, but, believe me, for Reading in 1964, she was far ahead of her time.

Was it my manly charm that had brought her here? I was once told that some women are powerfully attracted to cripples — and who was I to object? — only I'd yet to have it confirmed. I'd always assumed it was dreamed up by some guy with a game leg.

The hell with my suspicions. If you're male and alone on a Saturday night and a nineteen-year-old blonde arrives on your doorstep at midnight, you don't ask questions, you reach for the champagne. The Perrier Jouet was ready in the fridge.

I took a flashlight off the shelf and was on my way through the passage to the front door when I heard the creak of a board upstairs.

My bedroom. The nerve of the girl.

She'd broken in.

I was incensed. I'm sure it was a primitive response to my territory being invaded. If I'd had two good legs, I'd have been up those stairs and she'd have been out on her you-know-what before I'd drawn another breath. Instead, while I limped to the kitchen, my brain ran the gamut from outrage to arousal.

On reflection, I decided, I wouldn't throw her out. I wouldn't even register a protest.

She'd staked her colors to the mast.

I could be positive too. I took out the champagne and two glasses and put them on a tray. I'm fairly adept at balancing a tray on one arm, even when it comes to mounting the stairs.

I didn't put on the light. I know my way around my own bedroom in the dark. I leaned against the chest of drawers to the left of the door and passed my hand across the surface, prior to resting the tray there. Good thing I did, because my fingers came into contact with a pair of glasses.

Don't rush it, I told myself.

A trace of musk reached my nostrils and made me take a longer, stimulating breath.

I unfastened my belt and stripped. I approached the bed. As my hand touched the pillow, I felt her loosened hair lying across it. She'd unfastened the plait. I got in beside her. She was wrapped in my dressing gown for warmth. Our lips touched, and she guided my hand onto soft, yielding skin.

Coming up the stairs, I'd been thinking of the dustup if I'd brought Val home, as I'd planned. Now I stopped thinking about Val. Except that she was outclassed.

When I eventually got out of bed to uncork the champagne, Alice Ashenfelter spoke. Instead of telling me that the earth had moved, she said, "The catch on your toilet window is loose."

"So you climbed in."

27

She bit her lip. "Are you mad at me?"

"Do I look mad?"

"I can't see without my glasses."

I handed them to her.

She looped them over her ears and said, "A little *distrait* but not mad."

The cork shot across the room, and I filled the glasses.

My turn to look at her. The light over the bed put strong shadows under her breasts, parting the strands of her incredibly long, fine hair. I liked the hair loose. For a girl of, say, nineteen, the plait was a curiously juvenile affectation. Plenty of the female students I taught grew their hair long, generally wearing it loose or as a ponytail or, in a few cases, some form of bun. Plaits were definitely out. Possibly it was an American style that hadn't yet made the crossing, but I had the impression that it was special to Alice Ashenfelter. Her wide-eyed directness of approach went with it.

What I hadn't worked out was whether the schoolgirlish behavior was just an act or ingrained in her personality. A case of arrested development. But not, I thought appreciatively, in all respects.

As if she'd read my thoughts, she lowered herself in the bed and pulled up the sheet to cover her breasts. Modesty seemed to be reasserting itself, so I picked the dressing gown off the floor and put it on.

Now, I thought, for the price tag.

I sat in the armchair facing the bed and said, "There's something else you want to say?"

She raised her head and went through the motion of swallowing without having taken a sip. Then she said, with the reluctance sounding in her voice, "It's going to be difficult for me. You've got to make allowances."

I said, "The champagne is good for that."

"Okay, only please be patient. This means more to me than I can put into words. If I tell you why I came to England and went to all this trouble to find you, maybe you'll understand some of the dumb things I did, like letting the air out of your tire."

We seemed to be getting somewhere. I gave a judicious nod.

She pitched her voice lower and fingered her hair. "I want you to tell me about my daddy."

"What?"

"My daddy."

My skin prickled. What else could I believe but that I'd just made love to an insane woman? I tried to stay impassive, but alarm bells were jangling in my head.

"I never really knew him," she went on in the same intense tone, "but *you* did."

"Yes?" I said vacantly, then, collecting myself, "I think you might be mistaken."

"No. You knew him, all right. He was hanged for murder back in 1945."

FOUR

Things started to link up. With a jolt! The Old Bailey, May 1945. The Donovan murder trial. I'd been a witness. The papers had described me as "a pale eleven-year-old in a gray flannel suit who had to be repeatedly asked by the judge to speak up." Because I was a child, my evidence had to be given in the form of an unsworn statement, and the judge had asked most of the questions. In his wig and scarlet robe, hunched forward to catch my words, black, shaggy eyebrows peaking in anticipation, that judge still haunts my dreams. You can push an experience like that to the back of your memory, block it out with a million happier events, but believe me, it will not be forgotten.

The connection with Alice Ashenfelter was not so clear. The man on trial had been an American, it was true, a GI serving in Somerset when I was evacuated there. I knew him. But his name was Donovan. Private Duke Donovan.

As if she were reading my thoughts, she explained, "My mother married a second time when I was still a baby. His name was Ashenfelter. They changed my name at the same time.

30

That's who I am in the records and on my ID and all the documentation: Alice, daughter of Henry Ashenfelter."

"And he isn't your father? You're certain of this?"

"I have proof."

I didn't respond. I was trying to trace something of Duke Donovan in her features. I remembered him vividly. You see, I loved that man. Maybe there was something in the set of Alice Ashenfelter's mouth, the way her jawline curved, but it was far from conclusive. She hadn't convinced me yet.

She was uneasy at being scrutinized so minutely, because she filled the silence with more explanation. "I didn't know any of this until recently. I thought I was just like all the other kids, with eyeglasses and a brace on my teeth and a mommy and daddy who had fights. When I say daddy, I mean Ashenfelter, okay? Looking back, I don't think he ever loved me like a real father. One night they had a terrific scene over some woman he was seeing, and the next morning Ashenfelter quit. He upped and left us. I was eight years old. After that he never asked to see me or sent me a birthday card. When the divorce came through, my mother told me to forget him." She gave a quick, ironic laugh. "But we still kept his stupid name."

"He was one for the ladies, then?"

"You bet. The last we heard, he'd married again and gone to England."

"And your mother?"

"Mom was through with men. She devoted herself to me. She wanted to compensate for what had happened, I guess. She bought me beautiful clothes, sent me to riding school, took me on vacations to Cape Cod. We were real close in those days."

She paused. I was supposed to draw out the next stage in the story. Obviously the mother-daughter idyll hadn't lasted. Instead I asked, "What's her name?"

"My mom?"

I nodded. My memory functions on names. Ashenfelter was already fixed forever, but I needed something more evocative than "Mom."

"You mean, her given name?"

"Yes."

She hesitated. "If I tell you, would you use my given name sometimes? It helps my confidence."

I grinned at the notion that after breaking into my house, stripping, and occupying my bed, she was short of confidence. "I'll bear it in mind."

"It's Alice."

"I know."

"Hers was Eleanor. Everyone called her Elly."

I noted the past tense.

She picked up the thread. "Like I was saying, she was turned right off men by Ashenfelter. I remember on Cape Cod, we used to have fun sitting outside a beach café sipping Coke and watching the guys. We tore them into small pieces. We sure hated men."

"How old were you?"

"Maybe nine."

"And soon, boys were taking an interest in you."

She placed her forefinger on the bridge of her glasses and hitched them higher up her nose to stare at me through them. "You know what I'm going to say, don't you?"

"You and Elly fell out?"

"Right. The teenage rebellion. Preteen, and not just rebellion, full-scale hostilities, if you want it straight. The guys tried to date me, she got tough, and I blew my stack. Neither of us were quitters. She tried locking me in, hiding my clothes, whaling my ass off, all that stuff. But my hormones were always going to win out in the end, and of course they did. Don't get me wrong — I didn't get into any kind of trouble. I just got it established that I could go on dates whenever I wanted."

"And how did she react?"

"Badly."

"In what way?"

"Alcohol. Sometimes when I came in, I had to put her to bed. She had a couple of bad falls. One time she broke her leg, but it didn't stop her." Nervously she put her thumb to her mouth and pressed it against her teeth. "I'm going to cut this short. Last fall I started in college, living away from home. One morning in February I was called to the dean's office. Mom had been in an automobile accident. She'd driven off a straight stretch of highway into a tree."

"The drinking?"

"The autopsy confirmed it."

We observed a moment's silence.

I asked, "Did she ever tell you that Ashenfelter wasn't your natural father?"

She shook her head.

"In that case, how . . . ?"

"I'm coming to that. I had to go through her papers to see if she made a will. She kept everything like that in an ebony needlework box that once belonged to her grandmother. I found a sealed envelope in there. When I opened it, there was just a marriage certificate, some press clippings, and a few old letters sent by Forces' Mail. I glanced at the certificate and saw something unbelievable. My mother, Eleanor Louisa Beech, had gotten married in New York City, April 5, 1943, to a guy by the name of Duke Donovan! It really knocked me out. I mean, I was born the following February, for God's sake!"

She appealed to me with wide eyes, as if she had just made the discovery afresh. I muttered something inaudible, wanting to move on to other things. I'm uncomfortable with raw emotion.

"You think that was bad!" she said, inventing dialogue for me. "I took a look at the press clippings next, and they were really bizarre. Something about a trial in England. 'The Skull in the Cider.' Creepy. I didn't know why she kept them. I was about to put them aside when I noticed a name: 'Private Donovan, the accused.' Can you imagine how I felt? Jesus, one minute I found a new daddy and the next he was on a murder rap."

I smiled. Insensitive. I suppose I was as keyed up as she was, in my way.

Anyway, it didn't upset her. She looked at me with a glazed expression and then unexpectedly smiled back and said, "Do you mind if I call you Theo?"

I answered flatly, "You just have."

"Thanks. Well, I did plenty of thinking during the week of the funeral. I was very confused. I had one giant identity crisis. Either my daddy had been hanged for murder or I was Ashenfelter's love child. Someone had obviously faked my records. I could understand my mom doing a thing like that to give me a clean start, but I figured she ought to have let me know when I was old enough to understand. Theo, she never even hinted at the possibility."

"But you said you have proof."

"Right. It was in the letters I found with the other things. I didn't open them right off. I was scared. After the funeral I took them back to college. They waited on the shelf beside the clock, staring at me for over a week. I was extremely depressed, and I couldn't take much more. Then one morning I came back from a wonderful lecture on William Wordsworth that lifted my spirits. The sun was shining and I went straight to the shelf and opened the first letter. I want you to read it, Theo. Would you hand me my pants?"

Her clothes were folded over the back of the chair I was sitting in. I passed the jeans to her. She took her wallet from the back pocket and extracted a ragged envelope, which she held out to me.

I hesitated.

She said, "Please."

I took it from her and withdrew the letter. My own inner feelings were in turmoil. As I mentioned, I loved the man who had written it, loved him as a lonely child loves an adult who understands and offers support. I wanted to tap that source of strength again. His words — even to someone else — would be like a contact. But it was also a contact with a nightmare.

He had written in pencil on coarse, war-economy notepaper.

Elly, my dearest,

Another halt for the convoy, another chance to pen a few words to my sweet wife and our baby, trusting that somehow, sometime, you'll read them. As ever, I'm not permitted to say where we are, except someplace in Europe. "On the road to victory" is, I guess, a description that won't land me in trouble. I'm also at liberty to tell you that I still haven't been wounded, thank God. Weary, so weary, but not wounded. I'm going to make it,

36

baby, don't you ever doubt it.

Enough about me. Can little Alice say "Daddy" yet? I guess that's asking too much. There are kids here, would you believe? In the firing zone some kid in a bombed-out ruin asked me for gum. I always carry some. What'll we do together, the three of us, when I'm back? How's about a picnic in Central Park? Coney Island? And someday I want to take you both to Washington, show you the White House.

Stay brave, my darling. This comes with all the love in the world and kisses for you both.

Your own Duke

I folded it and handed it back. To be frank, it hadn't touched me as I had expected. It was a simple, dignified message from man to wife, and I had no part in that area of his life. Actually, it wasn't disappointing to feel uninvolved. It was a relief.

She was saying, "Beautiful, isn't it? I don't care what he did; that's a beautiful letter and he was my daddy."

I nodded, sensing that this was a significant moment. I had to be convincing now. Underhandedly, I slipped into her idiom. "Alice, you're so right. It's a wonderful souvenir to have. He obviously loved you and your mother above everything else. That's something to remember all your life. Why not leave it at that?"

It was a poor try, I don't mind admitting. She

37

showed how little she regarded it by leaning forward and asking, "How do you remember him, Theo? What was he really like?"

I said curtly and dismissively, "I was a child then. If you've finished your story, I'll take a shower."

But she persisted. While I ran the water in the connecting shower room, she argued persuasively (and accurately) that those wartime experiences must have made a lasting impression. How could anyone forget being removed to a strange environment and caught in a tide of events that culminated in murder and a trial at the Old Bailey?

I turned the shower control to lukewarm, which characterized my state of mind. For my own reasons I was extremely reluctant to dredge up the past. Yet I had to admit that Alice Ashenfelter (or Donovan) was entitled to know more about the fatal events of November 1943. Her knowledge of what had happened was fragmentary, gleaned from a few newspaper cuttings. Apparently she wasn't aware that she could have read detailed accounts of the case in a dozen different sources. The Donovan case was regarded in Britain as a classic of forensic detection. I had two books on the shelf in my living room that I could have given her to read. Murder being more commonplace in America, I suppose she didn't expect to find her father's case written up and copiously analyzed by criminologists, pathologists, and policemen.

I stepped out of the shower and reached for a bathrobe. I told her, "I'll sleep in the spare room. No offense, but there isn't room for two in that bed."

She said. "But you haven't told me anything, Theo."

"Want some coffee? I've had enough champagne."

"Please. I'll come and help."

"No need."

"Could I take a shower, then?"

"Of course."

I went downstairs and found the two books on the Donovan case and locked them in my desk drawer. Whatever impressions of me you may have formed up to now, I had no wish to cause unnecessary mental suffering to Alice Ashenfelter. I didn't want her finding a book with a picture of the victim's shattered skull on the jacket, and a mug shot of her daddy beside it.

I guessed she'd find some excuse to follow me downstairs, and she did. She'd wrapped herself in my dressing gown and tied back her hair with the ribbon she used for her plait. It was slightly damp from the shower.

She said, "I remembered my backpack."

"It'll be cold out there."

She ran out and brought it in. "You know," she said, "I have a bedroll here. There's no reason why I should put you out of your bed."

"Black or white?"

When I'd poured the coffee, I told her I'd found something for her.

She said eagerly, "What is it, a picture of him?"

"No. Just a souvenir. He made it." I handed her a figure about five inches high, carved from a piece of wood, representing a country policeman with his bicycle. On the base had been whittled out the cryptic words *Or I then?* If you examined the figure in a detached way, I suppose you might have dismissed the subject as kitsch, while admitting to a robust quality in the workmanship.

She stroked the carving with her fingertips, as if it were a living thing. "He really carved this?"

I nodded.

"And gave it to you as a present? He must have liked you a lot." She frowned at the lettering on the base. "I don't understand the meaning of these words."

" 'Or I then?' Written like that, they have no meaning."

"A secret message?"

I smiled. "Nothing profound about it. As a kid in Somerset, I used to meet the local bobby sometimes, and he always greeted me with what sounded like those words. It was the dialect, you see. 'Or I then?' "

She shook her head, still at a loss.

I articulated it for her. *"All right, then?"*

"I got it." She nodded, smiling.

As she still seemed somewhat bemused, I explained, "Duke was intrigued by the way Somerset people talked. He used to collect their sayings. Living with a family and going to school with the local children, as I did, I picked up a few examples for him. 'Or I then?' was one of them."

"And this was his way of thanking you? I love it."

"Keep it, then."

She reddened and said, "Theo, I couldn't do that. He made it for you. You kept it all these years."

"Duke would have liked his baby daughter to have something he made."

Her response was quick and spontaneous. She came up to me and kissed me on the lips. It pleased me. But if you're thinking this was the trigger for more steamy sex in Pangbourne, think again. She was still trouble, and I meant to show her the door in the morning. I didn't want a permanent houseguest. So, after the kiss, I put my hands on her shoulders and moved her gently out of range.

We sipped our coffee silently for a while, seated opposite each other across the kitchen table. She held the figure to her chest, as if it were in need of warmth. After a time, unable to contain herself any longer, she said, "You cared about him, didn't you, Theo?"

"Yes."

"He was kind to you?"

"Very."

"But you testified against him in court?"

I nodded.

After a pause she said in a low voice, "Won't you tell me what happened?"

I was tired and it was bloody late for a bed-time story, but she was going to draw it out of me before she went, that was certain. In humanity I felt bound to supply her with some sort of account. So it had to be now. I'm not much of a raconteur over breakfast.

FIVE

I'll tell you everything I told Alice. For brevity's sake I've decided to drop her surname now. I'm not sure when it was that I fell into the habit of using what she called her "given name." On that Saturday night, when my firm intention was to show her the door in the morning, I didn't call her anything. With hindsight I'm able to be more civil. You may think it unimportant how I addressed her, but there's a reason why I'm being scrupulously honest with you and anyone else who reads these words. You'll understand later.

This won't be a verbatim account of what was said, with all of Alice's interruptions and questions, because that would make it more difficult for you to follow the thread, but take it from me, you'll miss nothing you need to know.

I began by telling her about my evacuation in September 1943, the direct result of a German daylight air raid. A bomb, categorized in those days as high-explosive, hit the boiler house of our suburban school in Middlesex while we were singing "Ten Green Bottles" in the underground shelter, and Mr. Lillicrap, our harassed headmaster in his tin hat, was waiting white-faced for the all-clear. That same afternoon he was on the phone to his sister in the country. We were all given letters to take home. One notorious rebel, Jimmy Higgins, opened his and dropped it down a drain, but I dutifully handed mine to my mother. It proposed that the entire school be evacuated to Somerset the following Monday.

I think about half the children, eighty or so of us, finally assembled at Paddington Station, labeled and carrying gas masks, favorite toys, packets of sandwiches, and, in a few deluded cases, buckets and spades. In retrospect, I could have used one of those buckets. I remember waiting a desperately long time with straining bladder to file into a train with no corridor, for a journey of uncertain duration, and, somewhere west of Reading, furtively watching my flannel trousers turn a darker shade of gray. A couple of hours later, by which time I was surely not the only child with a secret (possibly even in the majority), we arrived at Bath Spa, only to be ushered onto a smaller train. Finally, long after we'd pulled down the blinds for the blackout, we were told to get out at a small country station in Somerset.

I looked at the station boards — I was old enough to read and proud of it — and informed my co-evacuees of our destination: Frome. I made it rhyme with *home,* which was comforting, and mistaken. Frome rhymes with *doom.*

We were marched in Indian file to a church hall where cheese sandwiches and orange squash were set out on trestle tables for us to help ourselves, while the public-spirited townsfolk who had volunteered to have an evacuee took stock of us. No wonder the bidding was slow. Even I noticed that we looked and smelled the worse for our journey. Some of the volunteers, I suspect, slipped away into the night, because at the end of the exercise the billeting officer was left with five of us (all boys) still without accommodation. Camp beds were found for us by the WVS, and we slept in a semicircular formation with our feet towards the coke stove.

In the morning we were driven to surrounding villages to be billeted with people who had no warning that we were coming. We watched dubiously from the billeting officer's farm truck as each door was opened and the earnest talking got under way. One or two must have put up a good case, because we moved on without leaving anyone behind. I was getting hungry.

We'd exhausted every possibility in Frome by late morning. There were two of us still without billets: a fat boy known as Belcher Hughes, whose glasses were held together with Elastoplast, and me. A telephone call was made at a post office and we were told that we would be the guests of Shepton Mallet. From the way it was put to us I got the impression that Belcher and I had struck lucky. Mr. Mallet, I confidently decided, must live in one of the large stone mansions we'd seen along the route.

We were handed over at a crossroads, where another billeting officer met us. My hopes of high living were dashed when I saw the names on the signpost. Belcher was allocated to an old lady in a terraced cottage, and I was taken several miles on, to Gifford Farm, in the hamlet of Christian Gifford, between Shepton Mallet and Glastonbury.

There I lost contact with the people I knew, apart from a couple of visits from Mr. Lillicrap. He seemed well satisfied with the instruction I was getting with the local children in the schoolhouse up the lane.

In justice to the Lockwood family, they hadn't volunteered to be billeters. They had to be reminded of the government's evacuation order. It was well known locally that they had a spare bedroom because their son, Bernard, had moved out, so they were obliged to take me.

My first contact was with Mrs. Lockwood, and my first impression was that she was a worried woman. She did a lot of head shaking and muttering in a dialect I couldn't understand. Thinking back, I suppose she was perturbed at the likely reaction of her husband to having me foisted on them. Much to her credit, so far as I was concerned, she started by taking me into the farmhouse kitchen and feeding me. I was given two slices of bread generously spread with dripping and gravy. The bread was fresher and less gritty than the national loaf we had at home.

Mrs. Lockwood would do me no active harm, I decided as I watched her across the wooden table nipping the stalks and stones out of victoria plums for a pie. Stout, with glossy black hair fastened with grips, and a broad face almost as dark as the plum skins, she was obviously older than my own mother, but she looked to be in better health. There were no dark crescents under her eyes from lack of sleep.

The inconvenient thing about Mrs. Lockwood was her voice, which was so soft that I had to ask her to repeat almost everything. Even then she didn't raise it a semitone. And as I had to repeat every utterance silently to myself to unravel the complexities of the dialect, communication was slow. It took the rest of the morning to establish who else was in the family and what they did.

Mr. Lockwood, I learned, had recently bought a smaller, adjoining farm called Lower Gifford for his twenty-one-year-old son, Bernard, who had moved out to the farmhouse a mile down the lane. The plan was for Bernard ultimately to manage both farms, when the work got too much for his father. The parents would see out their lives in the main farmhouse, looked after by their daughter, Barbara.

I'd already spotted one or two items of female apparel drying over the range that even to my inexpert eye would have looked skimpy, not to say silly, on Mrs. Lockwood. Barbara, I gleaned by degrees, was nineteen and worked on the farm.

She came in for lunch and captivated me without even noticing that I was there. This is pure Mills & Boon, but true. It was the impression she made on a nine-year-old who had shed silent tears in his camp bed the night before. Dark like her mother, though with softer skin and more delicate features, Barbara stood in the doorway and untied the green scarf around her head. A mass of fine, dark hair tumbled onto her shoulders. She shook it loose, talking all the while about something that had happened on one of the farms nearby. I was thrilled to discover that I could understand most of what she said.

Then she noticed me and immediately took me over. A few swift questions to her mother elicited the essential facts about me, and she picked up my suitcase and gas mask and showed me upstairs to the room Bernard had recently vacated. At the window, she stood with a hand on my shoulder pointing out chickens and geese and her favorite chestnut mare in the yard. After a bit we sat on the bed and I told her about my father being killed at Dunkirk and my mother doing war work and my Auntie Kit having us to lunch on Sundays. It emerged that Barbara had never been to London, so I talked urbanely about Trafalgar Square and Buckingham Palace. No one had ever listened to me with such attention before.

That night I didn't shed a single tear. I remember lying awake for a time, staring at the ceiling in my new bedroom, wondering about

Farmer Lockwood and what he would say about having an evacuee. He was harvesting, and that apparently meant that he would not be in till after my bedtime. At one stage I heard a man's voice talking seriously at some length, but it was the nine-o'clock news on the wireless. I fell asleep soon after.

Precisely when George Lockwood was told about me, I'm still uncertain. I have a suspicion that his womenfolk kept me under wraps for at least a day. My introduction was stage-managed. At four the following afternoon Mrs. Lockwood took a large basket containing freshly baked scones and a bowl of cream to the field where the harvesters were at work, and I was given the jug of cider to top up their bottles. Each man had a mug or a wooden bottle like a small tub, with a cork and an air stop. They kept me in heavy demand, excelling each other in pronouncing my name in what passed for plummy, middle-class accents. There were at least nine men and Barbara seated around the basket. Barbara's smile so beguiled me that I spilled some of the cider I was supplying to the man on her left. He reached up and grasped my arm, momentarily startling me.

Some of the cider had spilled onto his plate. He was the only man in possession of one. It was pink with a gold rim. This seemed a curious refinement, for he was easily the largest man there — six foot two, I would guess, with a mat of dark hair on his forearms and several gaps in his teeth. One of his eyes was bloodshot and partially closed.

There was something else about him that presently registered with me: He was wearing a tie. Not a special tie with stripes like Mr. Lillicrap's, and not elegantly tied. It was black and there were stains on it, but the wearing of it was a mark of distinction, for, I divined not a moment too soon, he was the farmer, my benefactor, Mr. Lockwood.

Still gripping my arm, he asked me something about the cider that amused the others and that I didn't understand. Probably he was commenting on my bad aim and suggesting that I'd imbibed from the jug, because when I politely answered yes, there were chuckles all round.

Mr. Lockwood released me and held up his mug to me. I believe he said, "Have a drop more, boy. Finish it for me."

Somerset cider has a notorious kick. Barbara tried to protest, but it was reckless to challenge the farmer's authority in front of his men and the extra hands hired for the harvest. He silenced her with a growl, still holding the mug with the handle towards me.

I won't claim that I felled my Goliath with one shot, but for a nine-year-old, I stood the test reasonably well. I told him I didn't have much of a thirst. I took a sip, felt the bite of the cider on my tongue, handed back the mug, and asked politely if I could stay and help and drink the rest later.

This met with general amusement and, more important, a nod from Mr. Lockwood. When work resumed, I was hoisted to the top of one of the trailers to help load the sheaves as they were forked up.

My memories are patchy. Little else of that afternoon remains. I think Barbara must have taken me back to the farmhouse when it was obvious that I was used up. She was certainly there at the end of the day, because she came into my bedroom and told me her father had said I could stay. She put out her hand and smoothed back my hair. I have a clear recollection of the touch of her fingertips.

After that the days blur, subdued by the routine of farm and school. I'll leave out my impressions of the Somerset education system. You want to know how I met Duke Donovan, and that's what I'm coming to next.

To compensate for my ignorance of country ways, I told a few tall tales to my classmates about life in wartime London, the unexploded bomb in our garden, the Messerschmitt that crashed into a barrage balloon, and the undertaker with the glass eye who was known to be a German spy. They hung on every word. The only enemy action they'd experienced was the distant thud of the bombs on Bath in the Baedeker Raids the year before. Otherwise, the best they could claim was an occasional glimpse of American forces driving through the village to their base at Shepton Mallet.

A few passing GIs didn't cut much ice with me. I was personally known to the U.S. Army. I'd been to a party — this part was true — at their base in Richmond Park. As the child of a war widow, I'd been invited there the previous Christmas for presents from a Santa with a Yankee accent, a film show, a singsong, and as much chewing gum and candy as I could stuff into my pockets.

Puffed up with the response this had from my new schoolmates, I bragged that I had so many GI friends that I could get gum whenever I wanted.

Fate has a way of dealing with braggers. My bluff was called sooner than any of us could have predicted. At lunchtime the next day we emerged from the schoolhouse and saw something that made my legs go weak. Across the village street, outside Miss Mumford's general store, stood a jeep in the light khaki color of the U.S. Army. I dug my hands in my pockets, whistled a tune, and strolled on nonchalantly, but I knew my number was up. They challenged me to get some gum.

Like the makeshift sheriff in a Western, told that Jesse James is holding up the bank, I crossed the dusty street, watched from a discreet distance by my schoolfellows. Someone shouted, "Through the door, Theodore!"

Inside Miss Mumford's, two GIs were buying drinks. The taller, who was Duke, was paying for a bottle of Tizer. His buddy, Harry, was eyeing the selection as if he didn't care for the colors. He asked for milk and was told curtly that it was rationed, whether you had it fresh, evaporated, condensed, or dried. No one tangled with Miss Mumford. She offered apples, but anyone with half an eye could see that her eaters had gone soft, so Harry said he wouldn't bother.

That was my cue. They were leaving the shop. Miss Mumford was staring at me suspiciously. In London I'd have called, "Got any gum, chum?" without even thinking about it, but I hesitated now, standing like a dummy as they passed. I followed them out to the jeep, trying to find my voice. Then I had my brain wave. I touched Harry's sleeve and told him confidentially that I could take him to a farm where there was fresh milk to be had. Harry glanced towards Duke, who gave a shrug and indicated with his thumb that I should climb into the jeep. I suppose you could say that with that trivial gesture Duke sealed his fate.

For me it was the summit of my career as an evacuee. I stood in the back of the jeep and saluted the troops like Monty in the Western Desert. We made a sharp U-turn and roared away, with me moving my jaws in a chewing motion.

The reckoning lay ahead. The wind in our ears was deafening, so I couldn't do any explaining in advance. I could only point the direction when the farm entrance came into view.

We swung into the yard with a screech of brakes and startled chickens.

I made a rapid assessment. Farmer Lockwood kept a small herd of Friesians, but I knew full well that milk was rationed. True, there was something called the black market, only it was against the war effort, and I doubted whether Farmer Lockwood was part of it. He kept a picture of Winston Churchill over the fireplace.

My luck held, because it was Barbara who came out of the farmhouse, alerted by the noise. She was dressed for riding, in fawn-colored jodhpurs and a white sweater. A look passed between Duke and Harry that she could have jumped her horse over. They got out and introduced themselves and were away across the yard with Barbara before I was out of the jeep.

She treated it all as a joke, as if asking for milk was a gambit just to come and meet her, and of course they didn't deny it. She blandly offered to let them take a pint themselves from her high-strung nanny goat, Dinah. The GIs wisely declined. Duke spotted a cider cask and said he wouldn't mind something stronger, to which Barbara responded that you only got cider if you worked. "Okay, sweetheart," offered Harry, unbuttoning his jacket, "so where's the work?"

Barbara laughed and said if they were serious, they could come back on Saturday when the apple harvest started. Some of the village girls were coming to help, and she reckoned her father could use extra hands. The GIs looked at

54

each other and said they'd both be there if they could get a pass. There were some jokes about passes that I didn't appreciate, and then they got into their jeep and drove off, still without the milk.

As Barbara crossed the yard with me she told me I was a scamp for bringing the Yanks to the farm. It was a good thing her father hadn't been around. If they turned up on Saturday, it would be up to me to do the explaining. I felt crushed, until she gave me a nudge and said, "Be fun if they do."

The harvesting of the apples, I learned, was a bigger undertaking than the haymaking. Mr. Lockwood grew many of the older varieties with stirring names like Captain Liberty, Royal Somerset, and Kingston Black. More humbly, there was something called a Nurdletop. Scarlet, green, and gold, they all went into the mill together to produce enough high-quality cider to supply several public houses in Frome and Shepton Mallet. Extra labor had to be hired for each stage of the process. So, I reasoned as I lay in bed that night, Farmer Lockwood shouldn't really object to the GIs. Even so, it was wise to broach the possibility before Saturday.

I took the opportunity the next evening. He'd finished work early and was smoking his pipe in his favorite Windsor armchair by the range. The smell of St. Julian comes back to me more strongly than our conversation. I stumbled through some kind of explanation, dreading that rural Somerset wasn't ready for my entrepreneurial efforts, when he cut me off with a comment that anyone prepared to do a day's work was welcome. As I came out of the kitchen Barbara gave me a large, conspiratorial wink.

The apple gathering started soon after first light on Saturday. Traditionally, women were hired as casuals and shared in the work, which was how I first met Barbara's best friend, the publican's daughter, Sally Shoesmith. Sally was a chunky, bright-eyed redhead with freckles and a wicked smile that may have been quite misleading. At nine I wasn't able to judge.

It was also my introduction to Bernard, the Lockwoods' son, who farmed Lower Gifford. I wasn't sure whether filial duty had brought him there or the strong turnout of village girls. From my point of view he was pretty unapproachable. My point of view was mainly his hobnailed boots, for his job was to take a ladder to the "keeping apples," like Tom Putts and Blenheim Oranges, that had to be harvested by hand, rather than shaken down by the polers. Below him, the girls jostled with their "pickers," bucket-shaped baskets made from withies. I think it gave Bernard a sense of power deciding which of his pretty entourage he would favor, from which you'll have gathered that I didn't much like him. He was handsome in a craggy, sunburned way, like a man on a knitting pattern. I preferred to follow the polers.

After an hour or so my ears picked up a distant buzz along the lane adjoining the orchard. It grew into a drone and then, thrillingly, the roar of the jeep. The Yanks were coming! I flung down my basket, dashed to the gate, and opened it in time for them to drive right in among the trees. To a chorus of delighted cries everyone stopped work and surrounded the jeep. Everyone, that is to say, except Bernard, who was stranded up his ladder with an armful of choice Tom Putts.

Wisely, Duke and Harry played down the excitement and showed they'd come to work. They were, after all, over an hour late. They joined in the job of arranging the apples in pyramidal heaps to get the frost before they were pressed. They were wearing what they called their fatigues, which amused the girls, who seized on every bit of service slang and every Americanism. To us all in 1943, the GIs were exotic beings who talked like film stars.

Speaking of films, did you ever see Henry Fonda in *The Grapes of Wrath* or any of his early movies? I mention this because to my eye there was a marked resemblance between Duke Donovan and Fonda. It wasn't just a facial thing. It was in the build of the man, his height, the head set on quite narrow shoulders, the impression he gave of being brave and vulnerable at the same time. His movements were unhurried and economical, yet there was a restlessness about him that showed most in his eyes. I think he was homesick. He laughed as much as anyone that day in the apple orchard, his teeth gleaming like Fonda's, but his eyes didn't join in the fun. His mind was torn.

In my childish illusions of romance, Duke and Barbara were ideally matched, and I expected them to be drawn to each other. It didn't cross my mind that he was married, let alone a father, and I'm sure Barbara didn't suspect it, either.

Things developed less smoothly than I hoped. When Mrs. Lockwood appeared in midmorning, carrying two steaming teapots, we all stopped for a break, and Duke sat at a distance from Barbara. Most of the men drank cool cider from the owls and firkins they'd filled at the start of the day, but the girls preferred tea. I noticed that one of the casuals hired for the picking fetched a mug for Barbara. He stretched out on the grass at her side, practically touching her. I learned that his name was Cliff and that he had no regular work. Sometimes he helped behind the bar in the local. I wouldn't have classed him as good-looking. Tall, dark, and unhandsome. All right, say it: I was a jealous brat.

The other GI, Harry, soon made inroads with Barbara's friend, Sally, giving her a Lucky Strike to smoke and finding bits of twig in her hair that took ages to remove. Harry was more the Cagney type, wisecracking and pugnacious. He told us he'd had three stripes and lost them for some misdemeanor. Harry worried me. I didn't want anything to go wrong.

When we resumed, Duke took a turn up one of

the trees, and I noted smugly that Barbara joined the girls working from his ladder. After a while she advised him to leave some griggling apples on the bough he was stripping. He leaned on the branch, looked down, and asked, "What's a griggling apple, for the love of Mike?" Barbara explained the folklore that any small apples had to be left on the trees for the pixies. Some of the girls hooted with laughter, expecting the GIs to join in, but Duke listened solemnly. Dialect words and country customs fascinated him. So Farmer Lockwood, who had a dry turn of humor, called out as he passed, "Come on, you lasses! Have Lawrence got into 'ee?" and Duke had to be told that Lazy Lawrence, the guardian spirit of orchards, transfixed anyone who tried to cheat the fairy folk.

Disturbing things happened in the orchard that September afternoon. If, like me, you don't believe in malign forces, you may think the cider at lunch had something to do with it. Or perhaps it was just the heady excitement produced by country girls mixing with American soldiers.

We'd gathered round an ancient wagon heaped with fallen apples of many colors, used to make the "windfall cheese" that would produce the first cider. The men sat on the shafts, the girls on upturned baskets, eating the bread and cheese with slices of onion that they'd brought in rush baskets and red handkerchiefs. Shafts of sunlight probed through the leaves overhead.

After we'd eaten, the girls showed the GIs

how to tell your true love with an apple skin, peeling it in one piece and throwing it over your head to see if it fell in the shape of a letter. Harry's fell conveniently into an *S*, and Sally kissed him amid shrieks of excitement, but Duke refused to try the experiment. They persuaded him instead to throw an apple high in the air, without telling him the purpose of the game. Several girls rushed to catch it, leaping like rugby players, but no one caught it cleanly. It bounced loose, across the grass, straight to Barbara, who hadn't joined in. She picked it up.

Someone handed her a knife. With everyone crowding round, she cut it cleanly in half and showed us two pips. The girls chorused, "Tinker, tailor," and I realized that this was a version of the fortune-telling game my mother had once taught me to play with plum stones. A boy was supposed to discover what job he would have in adult life; a girl would find out what her true love would be.

She took one of the halves and bisected it. There were no pips showing. She cut the opposite half. Someone (I think it was Sally) shouted triumphantly, "Soldier!" — but the word froze on her lips because the knife had cut clean through the pip. Apparently it was a bad omen. Barbara threw aside the pieces of apple and said, "Silly nonsense, anyway."

After lunch I didn't see much of Barbara. She was collecting farther up the orchard, with her brother Bernard, I believe. I heard one of the girls say, "It don't seem worth crying over," and the other gave a shrug and moved on.

Towards four, Mrs. Lockwood brought out tea and cakes and we assembled along the dry-stone wall where the sun was warmest. Sally was sitting in the jeep with Harry. Duke leaned against a tree, whittling at a piece of dead wood he'd found. I couldn't see Barbara, but each time a break was called, some of the girls would leave us to use the farmhouse toilet.

She still wasn't back when Mr. Lockwood gave the word to start again. I noticed Mrs. Lockwood look anxiously about her before she picked up the tray and returned to the house. A short while later she was back to speak to her husband. He handed his ash pole to Harry to take a turn and marched off into the thick of the orchard.

I sensed trouble for Barbara. Soon a figure appeared from the direction Mr. Lockwood had taken. It was the man Cliff, whose interest in Barbara I'd noticed earlier. He marched briskly towards us, ignoring some mild taunts about skiving. Without a word to anyone he continued straight to the wall where the bikes were lined up, collected his, and cycled away up the lane.

Then I saw Barbara coming from the same direction, closely followed by her father. Her hair was hanging loose, and she was carrying the scarf she'd used as a fastening. As she came closer I saw that she was crying. She broke into a run. Ignoring everyone, including her mother,

61

who stepped towards her asking, "Barbara, my love, what is it?" she ran through the gate towards the house.

Mr. Lockwood spoke briefly to his wife, and they followed Barbara.

At this point you'll be wanting to know precisely what had happened. I can tell you that Alice broke into my narrative and asked if it was a sexual attack.

I reminded her that I was just a child. If there was gossip, as I'm sure there must have been, they didn't let me in on it. All I know for certain is that Cliff Morton didn't appear again for the apple picking, and nobody would mention the incident in my presence in the house. I saw marks on Barbara's throat that I now know to be love bites, and I heard her mother's low voice through the wall, questioning her by the hour in her bedroom that night, but the words were inaudible.

Alice wasn't satisfied. She didn't seem able to accept that at nine years old I was clueless about sex. She kept insisting that I must have heard something, if not from the family, then from the village girls. If I did, it didn't make sense to me at the time, and I haven't retained it. I've told you the facts I remember.

Alice folded her arms and said, "I don't believe this!"

"All right," I told her evenly. "I'll save my breath."

SIX

She blinked rapidly two or three times, and her mouth trembled as if she were about to cry. She said huskily, "For pity's sake, Theo, don't clam up on me now."

I told her, "Leave it, then. I can tell you what I remember and that's all."

"But you must have thought about it since."

"Often."

"In that case . . ."

"My thoughts won't help you. Let's stay with my memories. Christ, we'll be here all night if we get into speculation."

Alice lowered her head and drew her arms tightly across her chest. "I've got to live with this tragedy for the rest of my life."

The self-pity didn't move me. I said sharply, "I was part of it. How do you think I feel, forced to go over it again?"

"Sorry." She straightened up and moved her hand across the table in a placating gesture. "I won't interrupt again, Theo. I promise."

I took up the story.

The stacks in the orchard multiplied during that last week of September 1943, and diffused sweet-sharp aromas through the crisp air. I joined the pickers at every opportunity, reluctantly fitting school and sleep into the intervals. While I was working, the homesickness hardly troubled me at all.

One evening after tea the GIs unexpectedly drove in to spend a few more hours with us. I was elated, especially as Duke had brought some chewing gum for me to hand round at school. The Yanks generally were known for their generosity to children, but to me it was more personal. Duke understood how I felt as an outsider. In between gathering the apples he asked me how I was treated there. I told him they were no different, really, from the kids I knew in London, except for the way they talked. He chuckled at some of the names I'd heard for ailments that kept them off school, like hoppy cough, brown kitties, and information. One boy had spent a week in horse piddle. Duke said he was collecting local words and sayings, and he asked me to listen out for more, not just at school but round the farm. No doubt he saw a small, lonely boy in need of distraction, although I know his interest in the dialect was genuine.

I've a suspicion that Mr. Lockwood overheard some of this, because as the light faded, he came out with a beauty, which I hope I remember right: "Well, 'tis dimmit near as dammit. Us be to home, I say."

Walking back with Duke and Mr. Lockwood,

I heard Duke ask after Barbara, who hadn't put in an appearance that evening. Mr. Lockwood gave a sniff and said, "Seen too many apples, I reckon."

"But she's okay, sir?"

"Right as rain."

Duke cleared his throat and said, "Some of the guys at the base are putting on a show for Columbus Day a week Saturday. Amateur talent, mostly, but not bad, not bad at all. Harry and I figured maybe Barbara and her friend Sally . . ."

Mr. Lockwood said as if the connection were obvious, "Can 'ee get hold of a gun?"

Duke frowned. "I guess I could, sir."

"Can 'ee use 'un?"

"Sure."

"Come over betimes. Shoot some of they pigeons for supper, talk some sense into my maid Barbara."

So a shooting party was got up the following Sunday. Four men with three weapons between them. Mr. Lockwood and his son, Bernard, had shotguns, while Duke and Harry shared a service-issue automatic pistol, a Colt .45. No questions were asked about where it came from. Acquiring it was easy, I imagine, compared with smuggling a jeep out of the base, and that seemed to raise no problems.

Being so young, I wasn't invited. I recall sitting in the farmhouse kitchen hearing shots from the woods and feeling sorry for the pigeons; needlessly, as it turned out. The shooting party shot nothing, and we supped on bacon and eggs. But the evening wasn't wasted for Duke, because Barbara agreed to attend the Columbus Day show if her friend Sally went too.

The day also ended happily for me. Duke promised to come back and show me how the Colt .45 worked. I might even be allowed to try a few shots myself. He was leaving the pistol in the drawer of the hallstand where the shotguns were kept, because there'd be another shooting party before long.

In bed that night I credited myself with bringing Duke and Barbara together. Two of the kindest people in the world; perfectly matched by me. They'd never have met if I hadn't brought Duke to the farm. I still reflect on it sometimes. The difference is that these days it doesn't send me into a deep, smug sleep. It has me racked with guilt.

On the night of the show Barbara brought me back a Hershey bar from the base. It was after midnight when she tiptoed past the open door of my room. I called out to her. She came in and sat on my bed and described every turn in the show, from a black jazz man to a man who took off Hitler. And she'd had the surprise of her life when Duke had gone up on the stage. He hadn't been on the program. He was just called up there to fill in with a song when there was some backstage hitch. There'd been a great cheer from the GIs as he went forward. They'd handed him a guitar and he'd sat on the edge of the stage in front of the curtains and sung three or four songs. He'd got a really fine voice and a great sense of rhythm and he'd written all the songs himself. The audience had loved it. And Barbara had felt fit to burst with pride when he'd taken his applause and come back to his place beside her in the audience.

She told me she'd be meeting Duke again. There was more to him than she'd thought at first, quite apart from his musical talent. Beautiful manners and a quiet, roguish sense of humor. Withal, he was shy, which she'd never have expected a Yank to be.

After that I looked forward to his calling often at the farm, but Barbara preferred to meet him secretly. Possibly she didn't want her parents to know how often she was seeing him, because there was a lot of local gossip about GIs behaving badly with girls. She used to say she was meeting Sally. I think Duke would meet her down the lane and drive her into Glastonbury or Shepton Mallet for a drink. She was always home before eleven. And I always left the door of my room ajar, in case she wanted to come in and talk.

Once, when I was cleaning my shoes outside the kitchen door, Mrs. Lockwood came out and talked to me about Barbara. There'd been some friction in the family since the incident in the orchard with Cliff Morton. I think they blamed

Barbara at least in part for what had happened. Mrs. Lockwood asked me if any of the village children had mentioned seeing Barbara going out with Americans. I was truthfully able to say they hadn't. The kids at school didn't ever speak about Barbara. Then Mrs. Lockwood asked me flatly if Barbara was seeing Duke.

It put me on the spot. I'd been brought up to tell the truth. Most times, anyway. Kids were fair game but not grown-ups. Lying to grown-ups was out. Yet I felt a pull of loyalty. Barbara was a grown-up, too, and I liked her best of all the Lockwoods. I didn't want to break a confidence. So I refused to answer.

To no effect. Mrs. Lockwood learned exactly what she wanted to know from my silence. And when I refused to confirm it, she bent me over the mangle and larruped my backside with a slipper for dumb insolence. She was a resolute woman.

It was the only time anyone struck me during my stay in Somerset. I'm not going to make the obvious comment that I was more surprised than hurt, because the truth is that I was surprised *and* hurt. That slipper really stung. Until that time I'd equated Mrs. Lockwood's temper with her voice. She'd tolerated me in her kitchen, fed me well, washed my clothes, and sent me to school on time. She hadn't given me affection, which Barbara supplied, but neither had she been hostile. Looking back, she was obviously under strain. She resented being stuck

68

with an evacuee and felt worried over Barbara, and it all came out as she wielded the slipper.

I'm grasping for a memory now. It's elusive, and I can't be certain whether some of it was wish fulfillment after my punishment. That same night I'm lying facedown in bed and the pillow is damp. I'm practically asleep when I feel the soft movement of hair against my neck.

It's Barbara.

I keep still, not wanting her to know I've been crying. Her face rests lightly against mine and remains there for some seconds. Then she kisses my cheek. The touch of her lips stirs me in a way quite new to me. She strokes my forehead, whispering that she's come to thank me for what I went through for her. She says I'm her little champion. She knows how much it hurt because she and her brother, Bernard, used to get it the same way when there was trouble, over the mangle, with the slipper, just like me. But they always deserved it and I didn't, and she feels ashamed of what her mother did. She promises me it won't happen again — not because of her, anyway. Before she goes, she kisses me a second time. That's all I've retained. I don't think I made it up. I can hear her clearly saying, "My little champion." Don't mock it. We were all children once.

In November the cider pressing got under way. The first frosts had nipped the apples lying heaped in the orchard, and we loaded them into trailers to be moved to the cider house. When I say *we*, I mean Mr. Lockwood, Bernard, and three farmhands, assisted between times by me and the GIs, who were eager to see the process. That's what they said, anyway. If they'd come to see the girls, they were in for a disappointment, for this was men's work.

Boys' work too. I was honored with a special duty. The old stone cider house was equipped with a loft, and the apples were brought there to be hoisted up in sacks through a door set high in the wall that fronted on the yard. It was my task, working by lantern light in the apple loft, to load the fruit into the wooden feed box of the mill beneath. I was given a wooden shovel, and when the mill was running and the word came up from Mr. Lockwood, I'd start an avalanche through the square opening in the floor, down through the funnel of sacking to the hissing, spitting cider mill. Tremendous. In the intervals I made a slide over the juicy, black mess on the floor.

Below me, the apples were converted into pomace, first by toothed iron rollers that broke them up, then stone rollers to crush them. Now Mr. Lockwood simply fitted up his all-purpose petrol engine. The pomace was collected in a wooden trough at the bottom of the mill and shoveled out with wooden spades. At this stage in the process, nothing of metal was allowed to come into contact with the fruit.

Beside the mill was a massive wooden press. On it, alternate layers of wheat straw and pomace were spread to build what Mr. Lockwood called a cheese. He stood beside it, shaping it to about four feet square, turning in the ends of the straw as each layer was completed. The final cheese was taller than I was, and they said it weighed a ton.

Then everyone gathered round for the pressing. Barbara and Mrs. Lockwood were called from the house. A tub was positioned under the press, the windlass was turned, and we all cheered as the thick brown juice gushed out.

The women hadn't come, as I supposed, simply to watch. At this stage they joined in the work, transferring the juice with wooden dippers to casks where it had to ferment. What really surprised me later — and the GIs, I remember — was to see Mr. Lockwood drop a leg of mutton into each of the casks. "Best cider's mutton-fed," he told us, swiveling his bloodshot eyes. "They bones'll be picked clean by Christmas."

One Saturday morning in the cider house, when the Yanks were in and we were having our morning tea break, Bernard made trouble. I'm sure it was calculated. He was malicious, resentful of the amusing turn the conversation always took when Harry was on form. He suddenly said, "Cliff Morton's been around again."

Mr. Lockwood looked up sharply and asked, "What do 'ee mean, been around?"

Bernard answered cagily, "No more'n what I

71

say, Father." His eyes were fixed on Barbara, who went pale. He was a sadist. He easily could have taken his father to one side and spoken to him in confidence.

Mr. Lockwood said, "Around the farm or what?"

Still with his eyes on Barbara, Bernard answered, "Saw his bike when I were walking home last night, didn't I? Stuffed in the ditch, far side of the north field."

Mr. Lockwood spat copiously into the straw. "If that soddin' bastard —"

His wife cut in, and I thought she was taking exception to his language, but no. "Blimmin' deserter too," she said. "Got his call-up papers September, I was told. Should've reported last month."

"Buggered if he's holin' up 'ere," Mr. Lockwood decided, on his feet. "Show me."

Bernard followed him out, but I don't think they found the bike, or its owner, because no more was said. Mr. Lockwood was back in twenty minutes to supervise the clearing of the crushed cheese from the press, ready for the next load. I helped Barbara fill a barrow with dry pomace for cattle feed. She wasn't speaking to anyone.

By lunchtime tempers were less frayed. The first cheese had yielded 110 gallons, and the second was taking shape quickly with the extra help of the GIs. When Duke and Harry offered to give me a shooting lesson with the pistol, Mr.

Lockwood told them amiably that there was no need to hurry back.

To my delight, Barbara said she'd like to join us. It was pretty obvious that she'd had a basinful of her family — her brother, anyway. Bernard had cynically and cruelly chosen the moment to tell his scare story about the odious Cliff Morton. It was calculated to embarrass and alarm Barbara in front of everyone. I think it had caused her more anger than distress. She was still subdued as we crossed the field to the edge of the copse where Duke had decided the lesson could safely take place.

We took turns shooting at an old petrol can. I learned how to load and take aim and hold the gun steady, needing both hands to control the recoil. By the end I was about equal with Barbara in hits, but neither of us would have been much use to the army.

On the walk back across the field Harry tried to liven things up by unfastening Barbara's headscarf and passing it to Duke. Barbara grabbed for it and missed. She was in no mood for romping about the field. If you ask me, she was still upset by what had been said in the morning. Duke held the scarf high above his head, fluttering in the wind, so that she would have to get close to reach for it.

Some girls would have resorted to tickling. Barbara was smarter. She grabbed the gun from Duke's pocket and pointed it at him. Harry shouted a warning, for this had become a dangerous game. Duke handed over the scarf, and Barbara slung the gun as far aside as she could and ran on alone. She'd had enough.

I remember that when I retrieved the gun and handed it to Duke, he checked that it wasn't loaded. None of us had been certain when Barbara pointed it at him. He still had a few loose cartridges in his pocket. He emptied them into the drawer of the hallstand when we got back to the farm. The gun was also deposited there. I'm certain of this, which I told Superintendent Judd, who interviewed me before the trial.

The cider pressing went on through the next week, and we didn't see the GIs again until it was almost over. They drove out to see us on the last Thursday afternoon in November, their Thanksgiving. I doubt whether the Lockwoods had ever heard of the occasion. I certainly hadn't, but I was highly gratified to receive as a present from Duke the carved figure of the policeman that I was eventually to give to Alice.

The GIs had planned a surprise. There was to be a party at the base with a buffet of roast turkey and pumpkin pie. They'd already collected Sally from the pub, and she was sitting on Harry's lap in the front of the jeep with her frilly petticoat showing. Everyone was in high spirits. I mean ourselves as much as the Yanks, because the last load of apples was in the cider loft, and Mr. Lockwood had shown his appreciation at lunchtime by offering extra cider from last year's vintage. The farmhands had been allowed to leave early, and only the family was still about.

For me it had been school as usual. Since getting back, I'd been in the cider loft helping Bernard and his father to mill the last of the apples. The mechanism made a tremendous noise, and I wouldn't have known that the jeep was in the yard if I hadn't happened to spot the movement through the open door. I jumped onto the trailer outside, climbed down, and ran to welcome Duke just as Mrs. Lockwood was coming out to offer them hot scones and cream.

First they wanted to tell Barbara about the Thanksgiving party, so that she could get ready. Mrs. Lockwood informed them in her placid voice that the two hours between four and six was Barbara's time for rounding up the cows and milking them. She'd started earlier than usual that afternoon, so she should soon be free, and she was certain to be excited at the prospect of a party.

I listened to this with mixed feelings, considering that it was little more than a month since I'd been slippered for refusing to speak about Barbara's meetings with Duke. The Lockwoods seemed to have revised their opinion. Duke's stock had risen rapidly since he and Harry had made themselves so useful on the farm. For her part, Barbara still wanted it understood that her occasional evenings out were spent walking with Sally, but I'm damn sure that if she'd admitted she was seeing Duke, there'd have been no objection.

I've sometimes asked myself whether I was secretly or subconsciously jealous of Duke. I can truthfully answer that I felt no animus towards him at any time, even after what ultimately happened. I couldn't dislike him. Between them, he and Barbara got me through what could have been the most desolate months of my life. Yes, I'll admit to a slight pang of rejection when they were seeing each other and I wasn't asked along, but that didn't amount to jealousy.

To come back to that fated afternoon, Duke and Harry went to look for Barbara in the field beyond the copse. The milking was done in the open air, from mobile sheds that were known as bails. The cows on Gifford Farm stayed out night and day, well into the winter months.

The rest of us, including Sally, made a start on the scones in the farmhouse kitchen. Mrs. Lockwood said she'd keep a second batch warm for the others, but it was never needed. After fifteen minutes or so, the GIs came back and reported that they couldn't find Barbara.

No one could understand why. She'd definitely said she was going to start the milking. There followed a confusing exchange between Bernard and Harry about which field they'd looked in, but as Duke pointed out, there was only one herd of cows, and Barbara wasn't with them. It was obvious to anyone that they hadn't been milked yet.

Mr. Lockwood said he'd take a look round after he'd put another load in the cider mill.

Quite soon we were all engaged in a search. Mrs. Lockwood ventured the theory that possibly the cider at lunchtime had affected Barbara and she was resting somewhere.

I'm not going to make a suspense story out of this. Things that happen to people you love — appalling, deeply distressing things — are difficult enough to articulate, anyway. I was the one who found Barbara. Some instinct or intuition led me into one of the smaller barns, set back from the main cluster of farm buildings.

At first glance it looked an unlikely place for her to be, for it was three-quarters stacked with hay. Then I heard a scuffling sound, too heavy for a rat. It came from the loft that extended halfway under the roof. Bales of hay were stacked there too. I couldn't see a ladder, so I used the bales as steps. There was a five-foot wall of hay confronting me when I reached the loft. By then I was certain there was someone behind it, for I could hear quite vigorous movements; so forceful, in fact, that I was discouraged from calling out.

I couldn't believe it was Barbara.

I worked my way along the barrier of hay and located a triangular space where the last bale met the angle of the roof. By squeezing sideways between the rafters and the hay, I managed to penetrate far enough to get a narrow view of the other side.

What I saw was my poor, gentle Barbara being raped by Cliff Morton. When I say raped, I'm using an adult term for an act that wasn't comprehensible to me at that age, if it is now. A violent, indecent, and humiliating attack by a strong man on a powerless woman. He was thrusting into her like a rutting stag while she struggled and gasped, beating her fists on the loft floor. Her blouse was open to the waist, and her overalls and knickers had been dragged down and were trapped round one of her legs below the knee.

There was nothing I could do except jump down from the loft and run frantically to find someone, anyone. Fate decreed that it was Duke.

He was coming out of the shed where the farm machinery was stored. I shouted to him that Barbara was in the small barn, and the man Cliff had taken off her clothes and was hurting her. Duke didn't say a word. He dashed past me across the yard to the barn. I ran on, crying, to the farmhouse where Mrs. Lockwood was talking to Sally, and blurted out what I'd seen. I told them Duke had gone in there. I couldn't do any more.

Mrs. Lockwood ran out, leaving Sally and me in the kitchen. After about five minutes she came back with her arm around Barbara, who was sobbing hysterically. They went straight up to Barbara's bedroom.

The only thing I remember about that day is much later, lying in bed. Mrs. Lockwood was leaning over me, giving me something to drink. I asked if Barbara was going to be all right, and she said yes, she would be all right, and I was to get some sleep.

They kept me indoors most of the next day. As soon as I got up, I asked about Barbara and was told she was resting, but I noticed that the curtains of her bedroom weren't drawn. That night I could hear her sobbing.

I didn't ever see her again. The next memory I have is the hammering on Sunday morning when they had to break down her door. And the screaming when they found her dead. She'd cut her own throat with her father's razor.

Later that morning my headmaster, Mr. Lillicrap, collected me from the house. On Monday one of the teachers took me back in the train to London and home. I wasn't evacuated again.

SEVEN

The rest is on public record, so if you're familiar with the relevant volume of *Notable English Trials*, or James Harold's *The Christian Gifford Murder*, why not skip this chapter? For completeness I'm going to bring the story up to date, but most of what follows will be second-hand, picked out from the evidence of police and other witnesses. My part in it was mercifully short.

I'll continue as before, reporting the facts as I told them that night to Alice. She'd kept her promise and allowed me to get this far without interruption, except a muttered "Oh, my God!" when I came to Barbara's suicide, which hadn't been mentioned in the press clippings she'd found among her mother's papers.

One evening in October 1944, almost a year after the tragic events I've been describing, a man in a public house in Frome, the Shorn Ram, ordered a pint of local cider, a drink strongly preferred in wartime to the watered-down stuff that masqueraded as beer. People didn't object to drinking from jam jars in those days of crockery shortages, but they were still choosy about what went into the jam jars. So when the customer complained that the cider was "ropy," it was a serious matter. The publican had just put a new barrel on, a large one, a hogshead, from Lockwood, a reliable cider maker. He drew off a little for himself and sampled it.

It's worth pausing to reflect that if the publican had been prepared to admit right away that the cider was off, Duke Donovan might never have been brought to trial. Yet these were days of austerity when you could be fined for throwing bread to the birds. It was against the war effort to throw anything away if there was the remotest possibility that it might be consumed. So the publican sipped the cider and agreed that it tasted more bitter than the previous barrel but adjudged it palatable. He carried on serving it for the rest of the week. Scores of customers imbibed it, but few came back for a second glass.

At the weekend, two of the Shorn Ram regulars went down with food poisoning. The cider was mentioned as a possible source of infection. Ugly rumors circulated of local cider makers who believed in leaving the bunghole of the barrel open after fermentation. It was said that if you looked closely at the sticky surface on the top, you'd see the footprints of rats. They approached but never returned from the open hole.

A Ministry of Health inspector arrived at the pub on Monday and took a sample of the cider for analysis. It was indeed "ropy"; not from the taste of dead rat but from contamination by some form of metal.

The hogshead was opened. When they removed the lid and poured the rest of the liquid down the drain in the yard behind the pub, everyone was expecting to find a metal implement in the lees that had collected at the bottom. Perhaps some careless farmhand had dropped a hand tool in there when they were fastening the lid.

What they found was a human skull with a bullet hole through it.

The process of identifying the victim is a story that has been graphically told elsewhere. Personally, I feel like wearing rubber gloves when I handle books about forensic science. Trust me: I'll rush you through the really gruesome bits. Suffice to say that the skull was taken to the forensic laboratory at Bristol, to be examined by Dr. Frank Atcliffe, a rising young pathologist who was himself killed tragically the following year in a civil airline crash.

There was precious little to go on. The action of the cider had destroyed all the skin, flesh, and brain tissue. There were no traces of hair remaining. Although the lees were sifted minutely, nothing else of significance was found in the barrel. Care for a glass of water? Or cider?

Dr. Atcliffe found that the skull was that of a man aged between eighteen and twenty-five. Mention sex to a pathologist and he thinks of mastoid processes and orbital ridges. And age is the ossification of the epiphyses.

Some newspapers mistakenly reported that the bullet had been the metallic agent that had caused the cider to go ropy. In fact, the bullet wasn't found in the cask. It had passed through the skull, leaving a clear exit wound. So what do you think caused the metal contamination?

A couple of dental fillings.

As Dr. Atcliffe later mentioned, had the victim possessed a perfect set of teeth, the cider would have been unimpaired. The cask and what was left at the bottom would have been returned to Gifford Farm for reuse.

Take a deep breath and let's deal with the bullet holes. The one on the left side, about one and a half inches above the aural orifice, was the entrance wound. The bullet had smashed through the right cheekbone on exit, just behind the eye. Dr. Atcliffe estimated from the size of the holes that the caliber was .45. It had been fired not less than a yard from the victim and not closer than eighteen inches. It wasn't possible to estimate the date of death.

The prospect of more grisly discoveries was widely discussed. Two more hogshead casks were opened and examined at the Shorn Ram, as well as a further seventeen supplied by Gifford Farm to public houses in Frome, Shepton Mallet, and surrounding villages. The publicans made no objection; there had been a marked falling-off in their sales of cider. But the casks contained nothing more sinister than bones of sheep. You and I might flinch at mutton-fed cider, but they didn't in Somerset in 1944.

The murder investigation was headed by Superintendent Judd of the Somerset Police, a God-fearing Glastonbury man famed for his lay preaching. People packed the chapel each first Sunday in Lent to hear him rattle the tin roof with his famous sermon on temperance. He despised the demon drink. He started his inquiry at the place he named with sinister emphasis "the source," Gifford Farm.

They said in the pubs that George Lockwood would be hanged, drawn, and quartered before the case ever came to court. Things couldn't have looked worse for him. The cask had his name on it. He'd supplied it in August. He'd personally hammered down the top the previous November. There were no indications that anyone had tampered with it.

George Lockwood was unable to recall anyone behaving suspiciously in the three weeks of cider making. Nor was he able to throw any light on the victim's identity. He listed his farmhands and helpers for Superintendent Judd. Each one was traced and interviewed, with three exceptions: Barbara, Duke, and Harry. Barbara, of course, was dead. Both GIs had left England in June 1944, to take part in the invasion of Europe.

When Judd raised the question of Barbara's suicide, George Lockwood admitted that it had happened on November 30, two days after the cider making had finished and the last cask was closed, but he could see no possible connection with what had happened. The coroner at the inquest had established that Barbara had taken her own life while the balance of her mind was disturbed. Judd didn't press any further at that stage but ordered one of his senior men to take another look at the circumstances surrounding Barbara's death.

In the meantime a check was made of missing persons, particularly young men aged between eighteen and twenty-five, in the Frome and Shepton Mallet districts. This wasn't easy. Some had volunteered for military service without informing their families; others had gone missing as deserters; and some had been killed visiting places like Bristol where there'd been massive bombing action.

But a list was compiled, and within days the victim was identified. Several lines of inquiry converged in a most convincing way.

The inspector who reopened the file in Barbara's death learned from the postmortem report that she had been two months' pregnant. Her sense of shame about the pregnancy, which she hadn't mentioned to her family, was held to be the main reason why she took her life. The identity of the man responsible wasn't established, and it wasn't a function of the inquest to name anyone. The family had been unable or unwilling to comment, but there were strong rumors locally that the man was Cliff Morton. It was said that he was obsessed by Barbara and pestered her frequently. On one occasion in September during the apple gathering, he'd tried to force his attentions on her and been ordered off the farm by George Lockwood.

Cliff Morton was a single man, aged eighteen. His parents had gone to live abroad when he was twelve, leaving him in the care of a maternal aunt who lived in a tied cottage a mile south of Christian Gifford. Two weeks after the inquest into Barbara's death, police had visited the cottage to interview Morton on another matter: he'd been sent his call-up papers for military service in mid-September and failed to report. The aunt told them that he'd left home suddenly without telling her where he was going.

So Cliff Morton's name was on the list of missing men prepared by the police. The age was right, and there was a connection with Gifford Farm. He had been employed gathering apples there, although so briefly that George Lockwood hadn't listed him for the police — an oversight he presently came to regret.

Detectives visited a dentist in Frome and obtained Morton's dental record. In January 1941, he'd been given two fillings in adjacent upper bicuspids that exactly corresponded with the fillings in the skull.

As final proof of identification, Dr. Atcliffe photographed the skull and superimposed the negative on the enlargement of a snapshot of

Morton provided by the aunt. If criminology is your hobby, you'll know that this was a method pioneered by Professor Glaister in the Ruxton case in 1935. The match was perfect. Beyond reasonable doubt, Cliff Morton was the murder victim.

The police descended on Gifford Farm in vanloads and began an exhaustive search. It continued for nine days. They checked every building minutely. They dug up the silage pits and dismantled the haystacks.

If you feel sorry for George Lockwood, I can tell you that he wasn't there to see his farm being taken apart. He was at Frome Police Station with Superintendent Judd, "helping the police with their inquiries." On all evidence he was better placed to help them than anyone else. He'd had both motive and opportunity. The motive was revenge for his daughter's suicide. He was convinced that Cliff Morton had got Barbara pregnant, and he didn't mind the police knowing it. And as for opportunity, Morton was known to have been hanging around the farm towards the end of November. Then who could have shot him, dismembered him, and put the head into a Lockwood cider cask but George Lockwood himself?

Lockwood admitted ordering Morton off his land in September after he'd found him "interfering" with Barbara. He blamed him for her pregnancy and suicide. He'd stupidly failed to notify the police that Morton had worked for him. But he denied murdering him. And he denied possessing a pistol.

Despite the thoroughness of the search, no further remains were found on Gifford Farm. Nor was the murder weapon discovered.

But the exercise wasn't wasted. After the bales of hay had been removed from the loft of the smallest barn, an alert constable spotted something embedded in one of the beams: a bullet.

Dr. Atcliffe was summoned to Gifford Farm, and he spent the rest of that day and the next alone in the loft, while Judd paced the farmyard like a dispossessed rooster. When Atcliffe finally emerged, he solemnly confirmed that a shot had been fired there. Forensic pathology is a cautious branch of science, but I strongly suspect that someone was being strung along. Judd blew his top, and Atcliffe waited for him to subside before announcing his second finding: traces of blood on the floorboards of the loft. The stains were not recent, and he couldn't say yet whether they were human in origin, but the pattern of staining, so far as he could trace it, suggested that the victim had lain for some time with the source of bleeding close to the floor.

Judd was all smiles again. Atcliffe smiled back and told him that he wasn't ready to identify the bullet. After photographing it *in situ,* he had sawn away a section of the beam and was taking it away for analysis.

The following afternoon he phoned through his preliminary report. The blood was human, from the group O, common to about half the population. He'd identified the bullet as a .45, of U.S. Army issue, probably fired from an automatic pistol.

That bullet turned the investigation on its head. George Lockwood was questioned for another hour and then allowed home to rebuild his haystacks. The suspicion had shifted to Duke. He, too, had a plausible motive. He'd been dating Barbara. It was an open secret that she was slipping out in the evenings to meet him. He knew about Morton pestering her.

Moreover, Duke had opportunity. He was around on the crucial dates. And it emerged that he'd brought a gun out to the farm, a .45 service-issue automatic.

Superintendent Judd hated GIs. If that sounds to you like unfair comment, try reading his memoirs. According to him, they destroyed our culture and seduced our women. The fact that they fought our war isn't mentioned.

He notified the U.S. Army base of his suspicions. The Americans agreed that there was a case to answer. They confided to Judd that Duke and Harry were "somewhere in Europe." To invite them back for questioning in the middle of an invasion was a practical impossibility. The American Army Criminal Investigation Department would deal with it at the earliest opportunity. This wasn't bloody-mindedness. Parliament had laid down a procedure under the U.S.A. Visiting Forces Act of 1942.

Judd must have gone spare with frustration. All he could do now was wait for the war to end. He went back to Gifford Farm and redoubled the search for the murder weapon and the rest of the body. The haystacks came down again, the silage was given another airing. Nothing surfaced.

I firmly believe it was only because time hung so heavily for Superintendent Judd that he decided to interview me.

By then we were into 1945. I'd been back in London over a year when the policeman knocked on our door. I'd come back from Somerset just in time for Hitler's buzz bombs. We'd had one in our street that killed six people. After that, Gifford Farm seemed like another world. I'd stopped crying over Barbara; our minds have ways of adjusting to grief. But I sometimes wondered about Duke. Everything had happened in a rush at the end. I'd left without seeing him. I had no idea how he'd taken the news of Barbara's suicide. I wished I'd had the chance to speak to him.

As I said, a policeman called. It was lunchtime, so I was home from school. When I saw the shape of the helmet through the frosted glass, I opened the door myself, remembering how it was a policeman who came in 1940 after Dunkirk to tell us that Dad was dead. I couldn't think of anyone else who might have been killed, but I didn't want Mum to faint again.

Instead of doing long division and nature

90

study with Junior 5 and Miss Coombs, I spent that afternoon in the police station. Superintendent Judd questioned me for a long time. He told me at the beginning that God would be listening, but all I could see was a lady policeman with a shorthand notebook.

I remember Judd for his shaggy brown eyebrows. They twitched a lot, sometimes together, sometimes independently. I must have given him a few surprises.

Most of his questions concerned Duke and Barbara, and I told him everything I've told you. I had no reason to be evasive. You see, he didn't say anything to me about the murder or his suspicions of Duke. I thought he was on about Barbara's suicide. At the end he reminded me that God had terrible punishments in store for boys who didn't keep His Commandments and asked me if everything I'd told him was the truth. It was.

Months went by. The buzz bombs stopped, and we kept hearing that the end of the war was coming. Everyone at school was back from Somerset. We had a *Daily Telegraph* colored map of Europe pinned to the notice board, and Mr. Lillicrap regularly shaded in the areas conquered by the Allies. When he announced to the whole school in assembly that General Patton and the U.S. Third Army had reached the Rhine, I had a strong intuition that Duke was with them.

One morning in the last month of the war, my mother told me to put on my gray flannel suit, because we were going to London. She wouldn't say any more, and I convinced myself that we were going to Buckingham Palace to cheer the king and queen because it was Victory Day. Instead we made our way to Lincolns Inn. I was shown into an office where Superintendent Judd was sitting with two American Army officers and a man in a wig and a black gown. It was a terrible letdown. They spent the rest of the day going over the same old ground we'd covered in my previous meeting with Judd. Before we left, they told me I might be asked to appear in court soon, but there was nothing to worry about so long as I continued to tell the truth.

On the way home in the train we had a compartment to ourselves. In response to my persistent questioning, Mum finally told me that Cliff Morton had been horribly killed in Somerset and that Duke was charged with his murder. The Americans had picked him up in Magdeburg and brought him back to England. After allowing the British police to question him, they'd handed him over to be tried under English law.

I was speechless.

I told you earlier about my appearance at the trial to make an unsworn statement. It's still disturbing to recall. I said my piece and answered the judge's questions, and that was all I saw of No. 1 Court at the Old Bailey. I was ushered out immediately afterwards, catching only a glimpse of Duke in the dock. I wish I hadn't seen him at all. He looked as if he'd been sentenced already.

I've read since that he was called to the witness box by the defense and made a poor impression, even before the prosecutor started on him. He was confused over dates, and he foolishly denied any attachment to Barbara, claiming that he only took her to the Columbus Day show on sufferance, to make up a foursome. He admitted that on Thanksgiving Day (the date of the murder, according to the prosecution case), he arrived at the farm with the intention of inviting Barbara to a party but insisted that he came out of loyalty to Harry, whose idea it was.

As for the rape, Duke conceded that he met me in the yard and learned from me that Morton was attacking Barbara. He claimed that he went into the barn to listen and formed the impression that whatever had been going on was finished, and he could hear no crying or sounds of distress, so he didn't intervene. He kept insisting that he had no romantic attachment to Barbara. He seemed more concerned about his reputation as a married man than about the charge of murder, shouting angrily more than once at his own defense counsel. It didn't go down well.

The court didn't make any allowance for his state of mind after ten or eleven months fighting his way through France and Germany. In fact, they turned it into a point for the prosecution, getting him to admit through a monstrously unfair question that he cared more about every

German soldier he'd shot in combat than he did about Cliff Morton. The defense objected, but the damaging admission was made. I'm afraid he came over to the jury as a callous man with an unconvincing story.

Here I stop, because Alice was outraged and wouldn't let me go on. She was incapable of looking at the trial in a detached way.

"Oh, for God's sake," she said, glaring at me through the glasses as if I had some influence over events. "If my daddy was guilty, as the court decided, he *couldn't* have been callous. He shot a man who was raping an innocent girl. Call that hotheaded, if you like, but it wasn't callous. British justice is iniquitous if it hanged him for that."

I tried to show her the logic of the verdict. "The whole point is that Duke wouldn't admit to killing Morton. If he had, there might have been more sympathy for him, but it couldn't have altered the sentence. His best hope then would have been with the Home Secretary, who had the power to commute it to life imprisonment."

She changed tack. "Isn't there something called manslaughter for killing under extreme provocation on the spur of the moment?"

Wearily (it was after two A.M.), I explained the prosecution's case. "They argued that Duke had a strong romantic attachment to Barbara. When he learned from me that she was being attacked, he rushed to the barn. On his own admission, he

94

didn't go up to the loft. He listened and decided that the attack was over. Then, the prosecution said, he made the decision to go to the farmhouse and fetch the gun from the hallstand, so there was premeditation. The delay put manslaughter out of the question."

She said, "Justifiable homicide?"

I responded unkindly, "Any second now." I'd passed the limit of my patience. I told her to give up and get to bed. I'd kept my promise and told her precisely what had happened, and I wasn't prepared to sit up all night arguing about it.

With much reluctance, plenty of ifs and buts, she finally returned upstairs with her rucksack.

I smoked a cigarette, collected some cushions, and carried them up to the spare room.

EIGHT

My mind was too churned up for immediate sleep. For at least a couple of hours I fretted pointlessly over things that could never be altered. And when I finally dropped off, it was anything but restful. I was a child again, being pursued by familiar ogres: Mr. Lillicrap in his black tin hat, blowing a whistle; Mrs. Lockwood, wielding her slipper and mouthing threats I couldn't hear; and, in a black Wolseley with a loudspeaker, Superintendent Judd, broadcasting a warning about the wages of sin. Whichever way I fled, whichever corner I turned, I'd be trapped in the Old Bailey with that staple ingredient of all my nightmares: the judge, leaning over me like a gargoyle.

I must have been reprieved towards morning, because I woke at nine-twenty, to the whir of the Kenwood Chef downstairs. My overnight guest was making breakfast. I'd firmly resolved to send her on her way by nine, but when I caught the whiff of fried bacon, I decided to compromise on a cooked breakfast and ten-thirty.

When I put my head around the kitchen door, she was turning a pancake. She'd dressed in her jeans and sweater and fixed her plait.

She said, "Hi. Would you happen to have any maple syrup?"

"With bacon?" I pulled a face.

"And pancakes. Sure."

"In the fridge door, I think. Will I have time for a shave?"

"All the time you want if you won't eat my pancakes and bacon."

I was an instant convert to the American breakfast. Between us, we got through a pack of bacon, five pancakes, the rest of the maple syrup, and four large mugs of coffee. Alice was bright-eyed. I commented that she'd apparently slept well, and she told me she'd taken a sleeping tablet. She'd been up since seven. Doing what, I couldn't imagine. The Sunday papers had arrived, and it was obvious that she hadn't opened them. They waited, still folded, beside her plate.

I naively asked, "How did you pass the time?"

"Rooting around."

I hesitated, rocked by the casual way she spoke. The acrimony boiled up in me again. "Are you serious?"

"Absolutely."

"Is that what you usually do when someone invites you to stay in their home?"

"No, this was special."

Her manner simultaneously angered and alerted me. I was ready to throw a fit, but I needed to know more. I said as casually as I was able, "Find anything of interest?"

She pretended she was reading the newspaper headlines. Without looking up she said, "Two books on the Gifford Farm murder that you hid in the drawer of your writing desk."

Still holding myself in check, I said, "And did it occur to you that I might have put them there to save you some distress?"

She looked up sharply. "Give me a break, will you? What do you take me for — some pathetic female out of a Jane Austen novel who might have an attack of the vapors?"

I said icily, "No, but I didn't take you for a snooper, either."

She ignored that. She said, "I found something else."

She lifted the newspapers. Under them was a gun. An automatic.

I froze.

She picked it up and pointed it at me, holding it firmly in both hands.

I said, "What's this, for Christ's sake?"

She answered with slow sarcasm, "You tell me, Theo. It looks to me like a wartime automatic, U.S.-made. I have the strangest feeling it's my daddy's handgun, the murder weapon."

I took a long, deep breath. She must have been through the house like a sniffer dog. I kept that gun in a metal cash box in the bottom of a filing cabinet.

I said, trying to sound as if we were still discussing pancakes and maple syrup, "You're right about the gun. Now would you put it down?"

She continued to aim it steadily and wordlessly at me.

"Alice," I said with more edge, "this isn't just stupid. It's bloody dangerous."

Her eyes didn't register anything.

I suppose I could have called her bluff and invited her to shoot. There was a chance that the gun wasn't loaded. The magazine and bullets had been stored with it, but they had to be inserted into the hollow handgrip. There was also the point that if she killed me, she'd be deep in trouble and none the wiser.

Would you have taken the chance?

That's two of us.

I made her an offer instead. "Put the gun down and I'll tell you about it."

She pulled the trigger.

From which the logically minded reader will draw two deductions: The gun wasn't loaded and Alice didn't care if I wet my pajamas.

It wasn't, and I didn't. But no thanks to her. I'm not proud of the language I used.

She lowered the gun slowly and rested it on the table. She found her voice again. The words, on a low, menacing note, owed something to old gangster movies. "Get this straight in your head, Theo, this is showdown time. This had better be the whole story."

It was a significant moment in our association. The threat of the gun had been removed, replaced now by force of personality. I had every right to take offense at the way she'd abused my hospitality. I should have booted her out. Yet I didn't. I can't say I was intimidated. Her tight-lipped aggressiveness was faintly risible. The reason why I played along was, now that she'd found the gun, I wanted her to know the truth about it. It mattered to me that she believed the whole of my story.

I warned her, "You'll need to think like a nine-year-old to understand this. Last night I told you about Cliff Morton raping Barbara, how I saw it happening and ran out of the barn and blurted it out to Duke. You remember Duke dashed in there. I rushed back to the farmhouse and sobbed out the news to Mrs. Lockwood and Sally Shoesmith. That was the end of my active part in what happened."

"You remained in the farmhouse?"

"Yes, with Sally. I was shocked and frightened."

"Did you hear a shot?"

"We wouldn't have. The cider mill was still making its racket. After a while the door burst open, and Mrs. Lockwood came through the kitchen with Barbara, crying out in distress, as I mentioned. After a bit Sally went out to the yard, and I went up to my room and remained there for the rest of the day. Through the wall I could hear Barbara crying. It was very disturbing. I remember wishing Duke would come up and comfort her, but when I looked out of my window into the yard, the jeep was gone."

"He left? What time was this?" asked Alice.

"I couldn't say. Before it got dark, anyway. I felt desolate. Later Mrs. Lockwood brought me some supper on a tray. It was difficult getting to sleep with that violent scene in my mind, and Barbara's crying. I'm not sure how long I stayed awake. I got some sleep eventually, because towards morning I woke up in a panic. I'd remembered something very important: the present Duke had given me."

"The carving?"

"I knew where I'd left it. I'd had it in my hands when I went into the barn. I'd put it down on a bale to climb up to the hayloft. I was in such a state when I came out that I'd left it there. The sense of loss was overwhelming. Duke had made it for me personally."

"You don't have to explain," said Alice in a whisper. "I understand exactly how you felt."

I'd touched a chord.

I went on, "I just had to get it back, and soon. A child's imagination foresees all sorts of catastrophes. I was scared of the dark, but I knew the Lockwoods were always up by five-thirty, so I had to whip up some courage. I crept out of bed and downstairs. There was a flashlight by the back door, and I was grateful for that. Even so, it was creepy approaching the barn, especially after the shock I'd had the day before. Inside, I could hear creaks and scufflings. Mice, I suppose. There was no going back without my carving, so I scrambled around, searching. I found it too.

101

But first I put my hand on something else."

Alice's eyes focused on the gun.

I nodded. "It was lying between two sheaves where it had slipped out of sight. Obviously, I decided, someone had taken it in there and lost it. You've got to realize that I knew nothing about Morton being shot. Now this is where you have to put yourself into the mind of a nine-year-old boy. That gun belonged to Duke. I'd found it for him. I wanted to return it personally, get some credit, you see, from the man I idolized. So I slipped it inside my shirt, and a few minutes later I located my precious carving. Luck was with me. I got back unseen to my room."

"And you kept the gun?"

"I didn't intend to. For the time being, I had it in the space below the bottom drawer of the tallboy in my room. At breakfast I asked whether Duke would be coming in that day. Mrs. Lockwood's answer came as a shock. She said it was unlikely if we'd see him again. She was so emphatic that I believed her."

Alice asked, "Did she give you a reason?"

"I don't remember any. People then didn't bother to explain things to children. So I had the gun in my room, and I'd never see Duke again. At the back of my mind I formed a wild idea of making my way to the U.S. base at Shepton Mallet and returning it to him in person."

She softened her mouth into the beginning of a smile. "I doubt whether he'd have appreciated the gesture."

I shrugged. "It hadn't occurred to me that he must have smuggled it out of the armory."

"You could have replaced it in the hallstand drawer in the farmhouse," suggested Alice, then added, thinking aloud, "But I guess it wouldn't have earned you the credit you were looking for."

"True. And I didn't want the Lockwoods acquiring it by default. But events overtook me. The tragedy of Barbara's suicide had swift implications for me. Mr. Lillicrap came in a taxi from Frome to collect me. I had to pack my things in such a rush that I almost forgot the gun. At the last minute I retrieved it from the tallboy, wrapped it up in a shirt, and stuffed it inside my suitcase." I spread my hands, inviting her to fill in the rest. I believed I'd dispelled some of her worst suspicions.

However, she was still frowning. "So what happened when the police came to London to interview you a year later? Didn't you tell them about the gun?"

"They didn't ask."

"At some stage you must have figured how important it was."

"Yes."

"You were scared of speaking up?"

"Certainly," I admitted. "But that wasn't the reason. I wanted Duke to be acquitted, even though he was guilty. I wasn't handing the murder weapon to the prosecution."

"So you kept it all this time."

"I had a loose floorboard in my bedroom. It went under there with *No Orchids for Miss Blandish* and some other secrets of my preadolescence."

Alice eyed the gun thoughtfully. "Are you sure it *was* the murder weapon?"

"It was the only .45 U.S. Army-issue automatic found at the scene of the crime."

My sarcasm rolled off her. "And it was loaded when you found it?"

"It stayed loaded until I got it home and learned the trick of releasing the magazine. There were five bullets inside, of the same type as the one fired in the barn."

She gave a nod. "I saw them in the box."

"That's it, then," I said with an air of finality, getting up from the table. "There's nothing else I can tell you."

I really believed I was about to show her the door. I'd scraped my memory almost bare, and it was a painful activity. I wanted to turn my mind to the present now. Just a quiet Sunday. The newspapers, a stroll down to the pub for a couple of beers at lunchtime, maybe some serious reading later. Next week's lectures had to be faced. And I'd probably find myself ringing Val when she came off duty, to smooth the ruffled feathers.

Alice stayed where she was, drawing a circle round the gun with her finger. I might have guessed she wouldn't be easy to shift.

I limped around the kitchen, tidying up, sourly

brooding over ways to evict her. I had the feeling that even if I yanked her up from the chair by her plait, she wouldn't take the hint.

"Want a lift to the station?" I asked.

I don't remember what answer she gave, if any, because I was distracted by the sight of something through the window: a red Ford Anglia moving slowly up the lane. It stopped at my front gate. Two men were inside. They both stared out. There was some hesitation, as if they were checking the address. Then the driver's door opened and there emerged a stout figure in a blue raincoat and one of those small green trilbys with a feather in the side. He peered at the house, made up his mind, and stepped splayfooted towards the front door.

So much for my quiet Sunday.

NINE

Close up, he was even more gross. Features obscured in folds of blotchy flesh. Wisps of colorless hair for eyebrows. As so often in fat men, the voice was the compensating factor, fruity as wedding cake, sonorous, confident, with a saving hint of self-mockery.

"What a salubrious place to live, sir." A quick revelation of baldness under the hat. "Digby Watmore, *News on Sunday,* and before you mention it, not in the least surprised that you never read the offensive rag."

I shook my head. "There's a mistake, I think."

The creases formed a pattern of excessive concern. "Mistakes by the million, sir, I'm the first to concede. But the blame lies with the typesetters, not the reporters. It pains me to see how they mutilate my copy, and I speak as a man who can spell diarrhea without the aid of a dictionary." He waited solemnly for me to react, his small, opaque eyes locked with mine.

Trying to sound tolerant, I said, "Do me a favor. Try somewhere else, will you?"

He didn't budge. He looked past me and raised the hat again. "How timely! The winsome

Miss Ashenfelter, from Waterbury, Connecticut. Tell me, my dear, is this the gentleman?"

"Why, yes." Alice confirmed it by stepping forward and slipping her hand around my arm. "I finally tracked him down."

Digby Watmore beamed his congratulations, then ran his eyes appraisingly over me. "So! The little evacuee grown up. Enchanting. It's a wonderful human-interest story."

I'd already unhitched my arm from Alice's. I said firmly, "As far as I'm concerned, it's no story at all. I don't know who set this up, but I want you off my property now."

He put up a pacifying hand. "Rest assured, my friend, we'll keep your address out of it. I don't even need a statement."

"You're not getting one."

"Merely a head-and-shoulders shot with Miss Ashenfelter. My photographer is waiting in the limousine."

"Piss off."

He stood his ground, unimpressed.

Alice spoke up. "Digby, would you mind if I had a few words in private with Dr. Sinclair?"

He dipped his head into his chins. "I sense that it might be opportune. I shall confer with the cameraman." He made a wide turn and retreated.

As soon as the door was closed, Alice said, "Okay, I deserve to have my butt kicked." Back in the kitchen, she stood in front of me, nervously tugging the hem of her sweater. "Theo, you've got to forgive me. I was so caught up in all the things you told me that I totally forgot Digby. I really planned to tell you about him."

I said ungraciously, "Don't bother. Just pick up your things, walk to the car, and tell him to drive you away. Now."

She colored deeply. "No."

It was like dealing with a defiant twelve-year-old, except that she knew I couldn't enforce my instruction.

While I stood dumbly with my blood pressure rocketing, she added, "Listen, Theo, you don't suppose I came to England and found you without any help, do you? I went to the newspaper, the one those clippings were from. They were really helpful. They tracked you down to Reading University and gave me an intro to Digby. He's just a local guy, a free-lance who sends them stories from here."

"And so incredibly cute," I said, aping her accent. "A wonderful English eccentric who wants nothing more than a little old photograph. Have you ever read that paper? It wallows in sex and violence. Your chum Digby's sniffing out a story here. It's old stuff, but he'll dust it off and give it a fresh slant. MURDER QUEST OF GI KILLER'S DAUGHTER. I WATCHED HAYLOFT RAPE, SAYS COLLEGE LECTURER. Is that what you came to England for?"

Alice countered with her own shaft of sarcasm. "So where would you have preferred me to go for help — *The Times*?"

"Clear out, will you? I've got things to do." I picked the plates off the table and carried them to the sink.

There was a long silence.

Then she announced in a flat voice, "If that's what you really want." She went through to the living room while I busied myself with the washing-up.

In a moment she returned with the rucksack hoisted, looking immense on her slim back. If you think I had a flicker of concern, you're right. I couldn't see how it would fit into Digby's car.

She told me, "I'm sorry I was such a drag, but thanks for everything, anyway. I can let myself out."

I nodded. I'd said enough.

Let's admit that I did feel a twinge of some-thing — guilt, remorse, I don't know precisely what — as I watched from the window. That heavily burdened figure walking staunchly out of my life was, after all, Duke's daughter. He'd helped me through the most difficult patch in my life. The fact that he'd killed a man didn't take anything from his kindness to me. He'd good-naturedly filled the gap in a small boy's life that a father's death had left. I'd loved him with the passionate loyalty of a son. And when my evidence had helped to convict him, I'd been sick with grief. Yet here I was, twenty years on, cold-shouldering his daughter.

I turned away, not wanting to look anymore, and slumped in my chair. I reached for the

Sunday papers. I heard the click of the front door as she closed it.

Although I had *The Observer* open and was scanning the front page, I wasn't reading it. Something was troubling me, and it wasn't just my uneasy conscience. There was a job I'd meant to do and hadn't. I'd finished clearing the breakfast things, hadn't I? I lowered the paper and stared at the blank, laminated surface of the kitchen table.

Then I remembered what I should have done: put the gun away. It was no longer there.

Alice.

Thieving bitch.

I grabbed my stick, hopped and hobbled the length of the passage, and flung open the door. She was already through the gate.

"Alice," I shouted, "you've taken something that belongs to me."

She hesitated.

I yelled her name again. I started after her. I could see Digby opening the car door. Wouldn't *News on Sunday* just love to have a picture of that gun?

Alice had started walking on again, without even turning round. She reached the front gate and groped for the catch, which was placed low on the post. Tricky, against the weight of the rucksack.

I negotiated that path in about six strides, angling my stick like a ski pole. I reached out and grabbed her arm with my free hand.

I said breathlessly, "I want it back. You've no right to take it."

She turned and gave me a cold-eyed look. "Who are you to talk about rights? It wasn't yours in the first place."

I said, "I made you a present of the carving. Isn't that enough?"

"That was something else," said Alice. "What are you afraid of, Theo?"

I didn't answer. Digby had hauled himself out of the Anglia and lumbered over to us.

He asked, "What's all this? Do you require the services of an arbitrator?"

I warned him. "Keep out of this." To Alice I said firmly, "Would you come back into the house, please?"

Digby said, "What is the young lady supposed to have done — walked out with the family silver?"

I said, "Sod off."

Alice was looking thoughtful. She asked me, "Can we do a deal on this?"

The words I'd used on Digby were almost out of my mouth again before I thought better of it. She'd outsmarted me. I wanted the gun back. If she handed it to Digby, my story would be head-lined in next week's issue: MURDER BOY'S 20-YEAR SECRET. She had all the top trumps. I was bound to fall in with her offer.

I nodded to Alice and tilted my head towards the house. We left Digby standing openmouthed at the gate.

Inside, she took off the rucksack. I moved forward to reclaim the gun, but she waved me away. "Don't come any closer, Theo. I have reinforcements out there."

"What do you mean by a deal?"

"I want you to take me to Somerset and show me the farm where it happened."

I screwed up my face in disbelief. "Why?"

"I thought you'd have my number by now. I want to find out what really happened at that place."

"I told it to you last night."

She shook her head. "Theo, I don't want to seem ungrateful, but I find it impossible to believe. I'm not getting at you personally."

"What's so incredible about it?"

She sighed. "Let's just consider the gun. You said you found it in the barn."

"Correct."

"So the murderer must have dropped it after he shot Cliff Morton, right? If it was my daddy, why would he do such a stupid thing, for crying out loud? He must have known it was vital evidence, an American Army automatic. Wouldn't he have taken it away with him, gotten rid of it someplace else?"

I shook my head. "He was afraid the others would see it. He was coming back later, you see, to dispose of the body and clean up the blood. So he tucked the gun out of sight, between two bales of hay."

She clicked her tongue in disbelief. "I don't

swallow that, either, but let's stay with the gun. He didn't pick it up later, did he?"

"Because I'd already found it."

"And you secretly kept it: that much I'm forced to go along with."

I said ironically, "Thanks."

Alice regarded me with that penetrating gaze of hers. "Theo, has it ever occurred to you that you weren't actually protecting my daddy by withholding the gun from the police?"

I frowned back.

She went on. "If you'd handed it in, they would have asked the questions I just did. As it is, they assumed he got rid of the murder weapon himself, like the ruthless killer they made him out to be."

A pulse started drumming in my forehead.

She said, "Disturbing thought, huh?"

I answered hollowly, "It's another way of looking at it. It didn't occur to me at the time."

"Because, like everyone else, you assumed Daddy was guilty."

"He was."

She simply looked at me and said nothing.

She'd made her demand. A quixotic trip to Somerset to prove her daddy's innocence. I suppose I should have seen it in her eyes the first moment she mentioned him. To my mind it was misguided and likely to cause us both unnecessary distress, but I was lumbered. I could see she wouldn't be argued out of it. The best I could do was get some safeguards into the contract.

I said, "If I agree, it's between you and me, a private trip. No press. Right?"

She nodded. "I can handle Digby."

"No pictures. Nothing."

"Okay."

"We go today and come back tonight. We can do it in under two hours."

"Fine."

"And whatever the outcome, you're on your own after this."

"All right." She held out her hand. "Is it a deal?"

I said, "When you return the gun."

She gave a slight smile. "I didn't take it, Theo. It's in the box in the filing cabinet where I found it. I put it back there when I went to collect my backpack."

TEN

We were on the A4, heading west to Somerset. Surprised?

By now you must have got me down as a hard-nosed opportunist, so I won't blame you for assuming I reneged on the deal after Alice made an idiot of me over the gun. Only I didn't.

I'd like you to believe it was because, after all, I'm a man of integrity. Duke's daughter had asked me to show her the place where the tragedy was enacted, and I was uniquely fitted to act as guide. It was a small repayment on my debt of gratitude to Duke.

I'd like you to believe all that, but you're sharp enough to see that she still had me by the short and curlies while Digby Watmore was in attendance. Who wants to feature in *News on Sunday*?

So I remained out of sight while she went out and talked to him. I'm not sure what was said. It took about ten minutes. The photographer got out to say his piece as well and looked decidedly annoyed. But Alice prevailed. Shaking their heads, the two men got back into the car and drove off.

When she came in, she handed me Digby's

card, which he'd wanted me to have in case I changed my mind about a photograph. She told me that he'd promised to keep in touch, and I took the hint. There was to be no ducking out of the Somerset trip.

I insisted that the rucksack traveled with us, telling Alice that she might wish to spend a few days in Somerset. She was a dream of a girl, terrific in bed, only, please God, not mine again. For peace of mind I was going to have to settle for Val, who went at it like a blanket bath but never mentioned her daddy.

For some while the only sound in the car had been the moan of the windscreen wipers working on a steady but meager drizzle. I can assure you that the weather wasn't on our minds. I was still stewing over Digby when Alice rather fazed me by saying, "I had no idea he would be so handsome."

I frowned. I simply couldn't see it.

After a pause she added, "I mean my daddy."

"Ah." My brain did some quick backtracking. She must have found those mug shots of Duke in the books on the trial that I'd tried to hide from her. Sad, wasn't it, that the first sight she'd ever had of her father had to be a picture like that? I don't know whether you'd agree, but I found it pathetic, really pathetic, in the old-fashioned meaning of the word. It was the kind of thing that gets to me. More touching, I think, because she was unaware of it herself.

I'd be a right bastard to abandon her.

I'm not a total idiot when it comes to women. I know when I'm being manipulated. For two days I'd been putting up a wall of cynicism, and she kept knocking it down.

She continued unselfconsciously and with a touch of pride. "I mean, it's not surprising that a girl like Barbara should have found him attractive. I can picture that first meeting between them, the day the two guys drove you back to the farm in the jeep. He must have looked terrific in his uniform."

I gave a nod.

We let the wipers take over again.

Sometime after Newbury she said, "The jury was out for less than an hour. That's not long, is it?"

"Not long."

Another silence. Her thinking was precise and unhurried. She meshed in her statements with the car's engine note, making sure I was listening.

"The prosecution had a very strong case."

"Devastating."

"All that ballistics evidence. I skimmed through it, but it must have impressed the court."

"Textbook stuff."

"They found some bullets fired from the same gun, right?"

"Right," I said.

"Where did they pick them up, Theo?"

"I told you about the shooting lesson Duke and Harry gave to me and Barbara."

"Oh, yes."

"The police combed that field and collected all the used bullets they could find and compared them with the bullet found in the barn."

Alice sighed. "And proved it was fired from Daddy's gun."

"Beyond any doubt."

After a pause she commented, "So they didn't actually need the gun to prove their case."

"Clever, wasn't it?"

She doggedly pursued her point. "It didn't make any difference that you had the gun all the time."

I said tersely, "We've been over this once."

She switched the emphasis. "All this forensic science, the skull and the superimposed photograph, the dental records and the bullets, sounds really impressive. The jury was bound to be dazzled by stuff like that."

I didn't like the drift. I decided to take a firmer line. "The case against Duke would have stuck without all that. He was guilty, Alice, there isn't any question. Listen, I know what I saw. After me Duke was the first to know about Cliff Morton attacking Barbara. I watched him dash towards the barn."

"You actually saw him go into the barn?"

"He ran in there. I'm sorry if this is painful to accept, but he really cared for Barbara. It was a crime of passion."

She shook her head. "To me it doesn't add up."

"Why?"

"He runs into the barn, right? This girl he really cares for is being raped. What does he do about it? Pull the guy off her and throttle him? No, he leaves them there and goes back to the farmhouse to fetch his gun. Is that the conduct of a passionate man?"

I said, "It's the difference between man-slaughter and murder."

"Okay, but how do you explain it?"

I sighed. "The prosecution went deeply into this. When Duke got into the barn, the attack was over. He could hear voices from the loft, Barbara pitifully distressed, Morton dismissing it all as unimportant. Duke was incensed by what he heard. He could have started a fight with Morton, but a beating-up was nothing to what Barbara had suffered. He ran back to the farmhouse to collect the gun, returned, and went up to the loft."

"And put the bullet in Morton's head right i front of Barbara? Is that what she told her pa ents?"

"She told her parents nothing. Duke sh Morton and covered his body with hay, ma pushed it to the back of the loft behind s bales until he could come back later whe one was about. When he did return, eithe night or the next, he had a plan. You have it from his point of view, as a serviceman v to join the invasion of Europe."

"He figured he'd soon be clear and a

"Yes. Obviously, his first concern wa get rid of the body. He could use th transport it somewhere by night, bury it or sink it into a lake with weights attached, but that's not so simple as it sounds. Digging a grave of any depth is more than one night's work, and how was a stranger to Britain going to find a boat and a deep, deserted lake? Even if he succeeded, bodies have an inconvenient habit of turning up. Someone walking his dog —"

"You don't have to spell it out," Alice broke in. "We both know what happened. He hacked off the head and put it in the cider barrel so the police wouldn't know whose body it was or how the killing was done."

We were making progress. From the way she was talking now, she was getting reconciled to ke's guilt. It was painful for her, and I under— her reasons for seizing on anything that nged the verdict, but she had to come to with what had happened.

ately, I *did* spell out the process of dis— the head. "There were twenty or more in the cider house. They'd been col— the public houses and scoured new pressing. They were hogs— familiar with the word?"

," said Alice, adding sullenly, night."

Huge. Over five feet high. You size of them to understand discovered when the tops After the top of a cask would be poured in through the bunghole and left to ferment. The cask wouldn't be opened for scouring for another year. By then Duke expected to be out of England."

"And he was." She was silent again.

We'd reached the stretch of the Bath Road to the west of Marlborough, flanked on each side by an awesome expanse of downland, profuse with ancient trackways and prehistoric sites. It can be an exhilarating drive, but this morning it was somber. We forked left on the A361. We were through Devizes before Alice made her next observation. It was a truism that might have been a line in a black comedy.

"I guess he lost all chance of a sympathetic hearing when he cut off the head."

"Fair comment," I admitted. "A *crime passionné* turned into a horror story."

"How did he manage it, Theo?"

I gave a shrug. "What do you mean, with an ax or a hacksaw? There were plenty of implements about the farm."

"He must have been covered in blood."

"There's no bleeding after death. He put the head into the cask and carried the rest of the body to the jeep to dispose of it somewhere else, somewhere clever, because it was never found."

If it sounds ghoulish to report that soon after this I suggested lunch, I can only insist that it didn't seem so at the time. We stopped at a pub in the center of Frome (not the Shorn Ram, which no longer exists) and had the traditional

121

Sunday roast with Yorkshire pudding in a snuggery where no one could overhear us.

Alice was persistent as usual. "One thing that still puzzles me is the reaction of the Lockwood family. They knew what happened, didn't they?"

"I couldn't say."

She was into one of her speculative phases. "They must have had some sympathy for my daddy. After all, it was their daughter who was raped. They may have kept silent so as not to incriminate him."

"Possibly."

"After the skull was found, Farmer Lockwood was under suspicion himself."

"Yes."

"And then it shifted to Daddy." She studied me intently through the glasses.

I suggested gently, "It might be easier to accept if you thought of him as Duke."

Sharply she replied, "I'll think of him exactly as I want. I'm not ashamed to call him Daddy."

I didn't react.

Alice hadn't finished. "We were talking about the Lockwoods. They knew Barbara was raped, right? They got that from you, and they saw the pitiful state she was in."

I nodded.

"But they didn't call the police."

"Apparently not."

"Why not, Theo? It's a criminal offense, for heaven's sake."

I hesitated. To be truthful, it was a point that

I'd never considered before. She'd forced me into speculation. "Plenty of rapes never get reported. Maybe they thought it was kinder to Barbara to spare her the medical examination and all the questions."

"Maybe." She pushed her plate aside. "But there is another explanation, isn't there? They knew Cliff Morton was already dead."

ELEVEN

Torrential rain on the canopy roof of an MG convertible is a sure conversation-stopper. It pelted down after lunch, all the way out to Christian Gifford. In these conditions I didn't do badly to find the village without a false turn, but I then had a problem locating the lane to the farm. I'd expected to use the schoolhouse or Miss Mumford's store to get my bearings. Both had gone. A row of new houses in that clinically smooth, beige-colored material that masquerades as Bath stone now dominated the center of the village. At the end of the row was a shop called Quick-serve with a stack of wire baskets outside.

The pub across the street, the Jolly Gardener, was apparently unchanged, though as a nine-year-old in 1943, I hadn't taken much note of it. All I could recall was that Barbara's friend Sally Shoesmith had been the publican's daughter. I stopped the car and went over to get some directions. The name on the lintel was no longer Shoesmith.

The barmaid, familiar only in the sense that she called me darling, obligingly came to the door with me and pointed the way. I didn't in-quire whether the Lockwoods still owned the farm. I wasn't pressing for a reunion.

Even when we started up the lane, it was dif-ferent. Where I seemed to remember the apple orchard were three large greenhouses. A gleam-ing silo soared above the hedgerow ahead. No trees at all.

I slowed the car and swiveled my head.

"Sure it's the right place?" asked Alice.

"Far from sure," I admitted as I swung the car onto a mud track pitted with tractor ruts, "only I don't see anywhere else."

Well, it wasn't exactly *Brideshead Revisited*, but I did get a prickling sensation at the back of my neck as a cluster of stone buildings swam into focus through the wet windscreen. Smaller than the picture I'd held in my mind yet more solid: the stark, gray-tiled farmhouse with the ancient cider house close by; the tin-roofed cowshed ex-tending past the end of the vegetable garden; the open structure that housed the farm vehicles; the main barn opposite the house; and, standing alone, the smaller barn of sinister memory.

"We've found it?" asked Alice in a stage whisper.

I murmured something affirmative and steered the car across the cobbled yard and parked be-side a tractor.

Alice flexed and clenched her hands. "I feel kind of nervous."

"Changed your mind?"

"Are you kidding?" She opened the car door and stepped out.

No one came out to ask who we were. We stood in the center of the yard with the rain lashing our faces. I waved my stick towards the honey-colored building adjacent to the farmhouse. "The cider house. Want to go in?"

"Sure."

I should have had the sense to realize that Gifford Farm ceased producing cider in 1945. In the local pubs jokers with a macabre turn of humor probably still talked about the days when you could get a drink with a good head.

The cider-making equipment had gone. The building had become a store for animal feed, and the acrid smell stopped us in our tracks. We stood in the open doorway.

"This used to be the meeting place," I informed Alice, nostalgic as if I'd worked there all my life. "On a day like this we'd all be in here, complaining about the weather. Sunday morning, it was like a pub, with neighbors calling in for a pint."

"My daddy was in here sometimes?" asked Alice.

"He parked the jeep right here, where we're standing."

She bit her lip and turned away. "Would you show me the barn where it happened."

I pointed to the small, gray building set back from the rest. "Sure you can face it?"

"Try me."

She took my free hand to trace a course between the puddles. She needed some creature comfort, and so did I.

Out in the yard, the rain obliterated the farm smells, so when I pushed open the barn door, the sweet pungence of hay was overpoweringly evocative. The place was still used for its original purpose, and the familiar dryness penetrated my throat and nostrils.

Holding my emotions in check, I told Alice, "It's just as I remember it. The smell. The way the bales are stored. Everything."

"It's darker than I expected."

"We'll soon take care of that." I let go of her hand and took out my Ronson.

"Be careful."

"There." I held the flame high, showing her the loft floor. A rustle startled her and she grabbed my arm. "Mouse, I expect." I felt a surge of bravado. "Want to go up? There's a ladder."

She hesitated. "Would you go first?"

"Of course."

I was glad I'd come. Here I was, inside the place I'd so often returned to in my nightmares. I propped my stick against a bale, pocketed the lighter, groped for the ladder, and hauled myself up. Hard work, but I wanted keenly to prove something to myself, and, I suppose, to Alice.

Flat to the floor, I leaned over and provided light again. She mounted the ladder fast and held on to my arm after I helped her. She was trembling.

Without my stick I had to put a hand on her shoulder to get upright. She automatically curved her arm around my waist. Disability can bring compensations.

I told her, "If you wonder how I got up here as a boy, I had two good legs then. The polio struck later."

There were fewer bales than formerly, and they were differently stacked, but I parked myself on one and tried to visualize the scene that November afternoon in 1943. I moved the lighter towards the angle of the roof where I'd found the gap to see through, and then over the area where Barbara and Cliff Morton had been lying.

Alice questioned me closely — in fact, it seemed to me, with excessive, if not prurient, interest — in the details of the rape, the precise position of the two of them, and their state of undress. She wanted to know if Morton was wearing trousers (he wasn't; the memory of his hairy thighs and jerking buttocks still nauseated me) and if Barbara's breasts were visible (her blouse and bra were forced up to her shoulders), if she was wearing scent (I didn't notice), and if her knickers were made of cotton or something finer (I ask you!). I answered everything as candidly as I was able, even down to the way Barbara had cried out and hammered the floor with her legs and arms as she tried hopelessly to twist from under him. I don't mind telling you that some of the things I had to say stuck in my throat, but Alice waited impassively until I found my voice and then coolly asked me supplementary questions. She wasn't held back by inhibitions.

We looked for the bullet hole and found a place at about hip height where a whole section of wood had been sawn out of a beam by the forensic expert, Dr. Atcliffe. Without seeing the angle of the bullet, we couldn't estimate the line of fire.

"Enough?"

Alice nodded.

Descending a ladder with my handicap is harder than climbing it. I was breathing heavily when I joined her. She suggested we sit down a moment on a bale.

"Was it worth the trouble?" I asked.

"It's not an experience you can evaluate," she said sharply, then, sensing that she ought to soften the remark, "But I'm grateful."

"What's next?"

"The Lockwoods."

"They must have left the farm by now."

"I'll find them."

I noted the change of pronoun. Up to now she'd been only too pleased to have me at her side. Was this an assertion of independence? Was my usefulness played out? Oddly, considering my earlier reluctance, I felt a stab of rejection. If Alice was going on with her absurd quest, I was beginning to want to be part of it.

I reached for my stick. "Let's try the farmhouse."

The wind whipped up the rain as we crossed

the yard. I thought a curtain twitched at one of the windows, but it may have been a gust getting through the casements. There was no response to our knocking.

I repeated, "It must have changed hands by now, anyway."

"I wouldn't bet on it," called Alice, already moving around the side of the house. "Look what I found — if the memory isn't too painful."

I followed her. She was by the back door, and she had her hand on the rusty mangle Mrs. Lockwood had bent me over when she slippered me.

I gave a mock groan. We needed some light relief.

"Any new people would have gotten rid of this piece of junk," said Alice. "Can you see inside the kitchen? Does it look the same?"

I got up close to check.

There was an instantaneous gunshot.

"Christ!" I said.

Chips of stone had been dislodged from somewhere above us and peppered the cobbles.

I asked Alice, "Are you all right?"

She was brushing moss off her sleeve. "I think so."

"Bloody lunatic!" I could see him across the yard holding the gun, a figure in a black oilskin and boots, standing beside the tractor, grinning inanely. I shouted, "What the hell was that for?"

I limped towards him, so angry that I gave no thought to the gun. "Did you hear me?" I yelled.

By way of reply, he spat copiously on the bonnet of my car.

"Peasant!" I said.

Alice had caught up with me. "Theo, be careful."

"Leave this to me."

I was close enough to recognize him. The face had thickened, and the black hair was flecked with gray. There were a couple of gaps in the grin, but it was still a strong, good-looking face that wouldn't look out of place on a Fair Isle pattern.

Bernard Lockwood.

I said, "You could have killed us."

"Rats."

I glared at him. There was no glimmer of recognition on his part.

He leered at Alice and said slowly, "I were firing at rats."

I felt like throwing a punch at him. I'm not incapable of using my fists. Without taking my eyes off him I said, "Alice, I think you'd better get in the car."

Bernard said, "Don't 'ee understand English? I were aiming at two old rats by the guttering there. Vermin." He made a creeping motion with his fingers. "Them as has four legs and tails."

I said, "God-awful shot if you were."

Alice hadn't moved.

Bernard folded the gun under his arm. "What you be doing here?"

"Visiting."

"Trespassing, more like."

I said, "It's bloody pouring and I haven't the time or the inclination to discuss it with you. We're going."

"No, Theo," butted in Alice. "Please."

"Save your breath," I told her. "The man's a thug." Perhaps I should have said moron. He seemed impervious to insults.

Alice told Bernard civilly, "Maybe you could help us. We want to get in touch with the Lockwood family."

Let's give him credit for some artifice. He didn't admit to his identity immediately, though it may have been due to sheer obtuseness. "Lockwood? What's your business with they?"

I said to Alice, "You see? We'll get nowhere." I really hoped we could beat a retreat without introductions, but she was digging in.

She explained to him, "They were the people who owned this place in World War Two, right? Are you the present owner by any chance?"

"Could be," conceded Bernard.

I'd had enough. I switched to the attack. "Come off it. You're Bernard Lockwood. Where are your parents, in the house?"

His hand tightened around the butt of the shotgun.

Alice turned to me in amazement. "This is Bernard?" She said it the American way, stressing the second syllable.

I was watching Bernard's spare hand. He'd taken two orange-colored cartridges from his pocket. I didn't have long to get my message across. I took a steadying breath and told him, "I was the boy evacuated here. The young lady is a friend. I promised to show her the place and, if possible, look up your parents."

Before Bernard could respond, Alice rashly chimed in, "My name is Alice Ashenfelter and my daddy was the man convicted of the murder here."

I could have belted her.

Muscles were bunching on Bernard's jawline. He frowned, grappling with what he had heard, trying to make the connection. His brown eyes darted between me and Alice. Finally, he abandoned the attempt and said through his teeth, "What's past is over. You'd best get on your way."

Curiously the words didn't carry the force represented by the gun. I risked an appeal to his better nature. "Come on, man. We've driven out specially from Reading. Your parents were good to me in the war. The least I can do is present my compliments."

"I'll pass 'em on for 'ee."

"Are they inside?"

I'd pushed too far. He snapped the cartridges into the gun, locked it in the firing position, and leveled it at my chest. "Get in the car and go."

Keeping my eyes on him, I said to Alice, "It's hopeless."

She evidently disagreed. "Mr. Lockwood, we came here in good faith —"

"Good faith be buggered!" Bernard cut in

133

savagely. "Bloody liars, the pair of you."

Alice protested in a high, accusing note. "That's unfair. I've gone out of my way to be honest with you."

Bernard sneered. "Honest? And you tell me you're the killer's daughter? And your name is Ashenfelter? You're no more Ashenfelter than I am, young lady. Name of the killer was Donovan."

I started to say, "That's easy to explain —" but Bernard talked over me.

"Ashenfelter was his friend, the littl'un. The other GI. What did he call himself? Harry."

Alice gave a gasp and grabbed my arm. "That can't be true. Theo, it can't be true!" She'd gone deathly white.

Myriad possibilities raged in my brain. For Alice's sake I said, "Sheer coincidence. Don't let it get to you."

She blurted out a rush of words: "Duke Donovan was my real daddy. Henry Ashenfelter was the man my mother married in 1947, when I was a kid. I was given his name. If he was Duke's friend Harry, I figure he came back from the war and married my mom."

Bernard looked unimpressed. "Good try, miss. Not good enough. Ashenfelter married Sally Shoesmith."

I said, "Barbara's friend?"

"You'd remember if you were here. They were courting like cats in heat."

"And they actually married?"

134

"Live in Bath like a lord and lady, don't they? Publican's daughter, that's all she were, and now you need a bloody visiting card to speak to her." He grinned slyly. "Not that you'd get much sense out of her, from what I've heard."

"Is something the matter with Sally, then?"

He spat again, aiming it at my shoes. "Clear off. Bloody liars."

Alice said in a choking voice, "Theo, let's go."

I took a step backwards, nodding to Bernard.

He lowered the gun.

We drove away without another word.

TWELVE

Alice sighed and said, "I just don't understand."

She said it again, twice, before we reached the end of the lane.

I pulled off the road outside the Jolly Gardener, switched off, and turned to look at her. Until that moment I hadn't appreciated what a soaking we'd both taken. Her hair was so saturated that you'd never have known she was normally a blonde.

She blinked. The drops of moisture on her cheeks might have rolled off her head, but I wasn't certain. The edges of her eyes and mouth were creased with worry. She tried to form a word and didn't succeed. She was obviously deeply troubled.

I wasn't a picture of serenity myself. I'd never met a woman who triggered such conflicting responses in me.

I took her hand. She was cold, as much from shock, I decided, as exposure. I told her with gentle authority, "There's a log fire in the pub. I'm taking you in there to dry out."

It was near closing time and the barmaid was

clearing the empties, but she seemed genuinely pleased to see us. I don't think she was run off her feet. The clientele consisted of two motionless old men perched on stools at opposite ends of the bar. Without consulting Alice I ordered two double brandies and carried them to the fireplace. The barmaid — did I mention that she was a pretty, dark-haired woman in her thirties? — followed me over, fussed sympathetically about our sodden clothes, and set to work with the poker to coax more activity from the fire. She wanted to know if we'd found the farm and I thanked her. If she was expecting some gossip about the Lockwoods, she was disappointed. Instead I asked if we could borrow a towel for Alice's hair.

There's a lot to be said for real flames and the smell of charred wood. It was a wide, stone-built fireplace with an iron pot-crane, a pair of dusty bellows, and a paved hearth. We flopped gratefully into a well-scuffed leather settee already occupied by two black-and-white cats. Alice removed her glasses, uncoiled her plait, and leaned forward, letting the damp hair get the benefit of the heat.

The barmaid returned and handed the towel to me with a wink and a firm instruction not to handle the young lady too roughly. It would have been churlish after that to pass the towel to Alice, so without discussing it I applied myself to the task and gradually restored some of the softness to her hair.

Presently she took out a comb and worked silently on the job of easing out the tangles. I sat back, sipping the brandy, and spoke the words of reason I'd been rehearsing as I used the towel. "Don't you think you're getting sidetracked? Does it really matter a tinker's cuss about Harry? He's unimportant."

She stopped the combing and lowered her eyelids in a way that made me wish I'd phrased it more sensitively. I was treating her like one of my second-year students who'd messed up an essay on the feudal system. Without her glasses and with her hair unfastened like this — you're right, girls, I'm a dyed-in-the-wool chauvinist — she was an extremely appealing woman.

I made another stab. "Alice, I can see you're going to suffer until you make sense of what we've heard. I'm not pressing, but if it would help to talk it over . . ."

She lifted her face and said, "Please, Theo."

You can put it down to the firelight, or the brandy, or the clear blue trust in her eyes, but if there was a moment in our association when it promised to become a relationship, this, for me, was it. I wanted her.

There was a short hiatus before I marshaled my thoughts sufficiently to say, "All right. Let's compare notes on Harry the GI and your stepfather. See if we're talking about the same guy. Harry must have been slightly older than Duke, say about twenty-five in 1943. He'd put in a few more years of service and made a sergeant's rank, then lost his stripes over some disciplinary thing."

"The age is spot on," Alice confirmed. "Henry was twenty-nine when he married Mom."

"Short — say five-five — thickset with sandy-colored, crinkly hair?"

"Mm." She frowned, concentrating hard. "Stubby, nicotine-stained fingers with small, pinched-in nails that looked ingrowing?"

"Snap." I'd watched Harry use those repulsive little hands to pick leaves and pieces of twig from Sally's hair. "Do we need to go on?"

Alice shook her head. "I don't need any more convincing. I can see how it happened. Harry is my daddy's buddy. When he gets back to the States after the war, he calls on Mom to pay his respects, offer her some words of comfort. She's feeling really low, a widow at twenty-two with a baby to bring up. She can't even say her man died with honor. She can't meet with other war widows, and she doesn't qualify for a pension. Is it any wonder she grabbed the chance of marrying Harry?"

"Is it any wonder that it didn't work out?"

She stared fixedly into the flames. "I don't care if he was my daddy's buddy. He was a schmuck."

After an interval I said, "When did Harry abandon her?"

"I was eight years old. 1952."

"I think you told me he came to England and married a second time."

She swung around to face me with wide, astonished eyes. "He must have come over here to look for Sally, his wartime romance. Theo, is that what happened, do you think?"

"Let's find out if we can." I turned and looked towards the bar. One of the old men had gone.

"Last orders, my love?" called the barmaid.

Neither of us had finished the brandy. "No, thanks, but you may be able to help us. Some people called Shoesmith had this pub in the war."

The barmaid nodded. "Right up to the fifties, I believe. What year was the Coronation?"

"Did you know them?"

"Everyone knew the Shoesmiths. They were a village family. Been here for generations."

"Gone now?"

She crossed herself and said, "Gathered, my love. The parents, I mean. Sally the daughter is still going, after a fashion."

"What does that mean?"

The barmaid looked away. "Gossip, my love, just gossip. She got married and lives in Bath."

"So we heard. To an American."

She was obviously glad to move on to someone else. "A real live wire, he is. And saucy with it. Comes in here regular and takes all sorts of liberties. Wandering hands, you know? He's in the antique business and does very nicely out of it, thank you, a white Mercedes and a house in the Royal Crescent, so he can afford to buy me a martini when I take offense, which I do, naturally."

I smiled back. "Any idea which year he married Sally?"

"The same year the family gave up the pub. That was a summer for parties. We had the Coronation and the wedding reception and the farewell do."

"1953," the old man unexpectedly contributed.

I looked at Alice.

She'd replaced her glasses. She studied me through them as if making up her mind. "Theo?"

"Yes?"

"I don't believe I can face Harry alone."

"Do you need to?"

A sigh. "It's essential. He must know all the answers."

"You want me to take you to Bath?"

On the way out I thanked the barmaid and bought her a martini. The old man perked up and said his was a pint of Usher's, probably the easiest he'd earned since Coronation year.

THIRTEEN

As a medievalist, I don't mind telling you that Bath's much-vaunted Georgian architecture leaves me cold. I find it crushingly dull. In my two years as a Ph.D. student at Bristol I visited Bath (a twenty-minute train ride) not more than three times, and then only for the secondhand bookshops.

Yet this October evening, driving towards the city at dusk with Alice beside me, I saw it from the height of the downs on the south side and was captivated. I stopped the car, and we got out for a better view. A shaft of orange sunlight had penetrated the purple cloud and picked out the intricate levels of buildings with dazzling clarity. From the shadows of the surrounding hills, beady rows of street lamps converged on the floodlit Abbey.

I was standing close to Alice. She hadn't bothered to fix her plait since we left the pub, and a few stray hairs stirred and brushed my cheek. I slid my hand around hers and locked fingers with her. As she turned to speak, I lowered my face to kiss her.

She backed away as if I had the plague.

This was the girl who the previous night had stripped and waited in my bed for me.

"What's up?" I asked her.

"I don't want to." She took another step back.

I smiled and made light of it. "I don't mind playing kiss and run, but not to these rules."

She reddened. "What do you mean?"

"Just take it easy."

She tugged severely at her hair and explained, "I hate to be a drag, but I can't relax while there's so much on my mind."

So we got back in the car and drove down the hill into Bath. I don't force myself on women, and I don't beg, either. Dismiss it, I thought. Yet it bothered me.

There wasn't time to speculate. We were in the Circus, approaching the Royal Crescent, and we hadn't yet made any ground rules for the meeting with the Ashenfelters. I didn't expect them to come at us with a shotgun, but I could foresee mayhem if Alice started laying into Harry for abandoning her mom. I took an extra turn around the Circus before we moved into Brock Street.

"About these people," I said. "Let's remember that they haven't seen either of us since we were kids. Why don't you keep in the background to start with?"

"You mean, not say who I am?"

"You don't need to volunteer the information. It might get us off on the wrong tack."

She said dubiously, "It seems kind of devious.

I like to be straight with people."

"Like you were when you brought your tray to my table in Ernestine's Restaurant?"

She protested with a harsh intake of breath. "I told you my name."

"And how much else?"

"I needed to get to know you first."

"Get my confidence."

"Well, yes, but . . ." Her voice trailed away.

I laid it out for her. "What it comes down to, Alice, is what you want to get out of this meeting — assuming they agree to talk to us at all. If you want a family reunion, that's up to you, but if you're hoping for some insights into Duke's behavior in 1943, I suggest you play it my way."

After a pause for thought she murmured, "Okay."

I've already pulled the plug on Bath, so to speak, so I won't knock the Crescent. For anyone who hasn't been there, it's built on high ground with a view of the city across open parkland. A single block of thirty three-story houses in an elliptical curve, with a facade of 114 Ionic columns and a roof-level balustrade. Enough said?

We bumped over the cobbled roadway and parked under a street lamp on the far side. Alice confirmed that there was a light behind Harry's blinds.

Harry himself came down to answer the bell.

I apologized for disturbing him, explained

144

that we'd driven over from Christian Gifford and that I was the boy evacuee he and Duke had befriended in 1943.

It wasn't the admission ticket I'd hoped it might be.

"Is that a fact?" said Harry without a glimmer of interest. The years had creased the Cagney profile into something closer to Edward G. Robinson. Some sagging about the eyes, more weight on the jowls, less hair, and thick-rimmed bifocals. He'd never been much to look at, but the saving sense of fun had vanished. He was in leather carpet slippers, fawn trousers, and a thick brown cardigan.

"A bloody awful time for all of us," I said, plowing on. "I can tell you, I was more than grateful for the kindness you fellows showed me."

"So?"

"So when I heard that you lived in Bath, I thought I couldn't go by without calling on the off-chance that you were in." I was beginning to feel, and sound, like a door-to-door salesman.

"Who told you I was here?" asked Harry, as if he meant to throttle them.

"The people in the pub. They said you came back to England after the war to marry Sally. How is she, by the way?"

His stubby hand cupped his chin in a defensive gesture. "You know Sally?"

"We all picked apples together, didn't we?"

My first question had given him a let-out.

"She's not so good, so you won't mind if I don't invite you in."

I was on the point of cutting my losses and pushing Alice forward with her guess-who-I-am speech when a woman's voice from inside called, "Who is it, Harry?" and Sally appeared in the hall in a white housecoat and swansdown mules.

I assumed it was Sally. She wore dark glasses, and her red hair had taken on a synthetic orangey hue. Unlike Harry, she'd shed weight since the apple-orchard days. Too much: I'd say she looked gaunt.

Harry held on to the door and said over his shoulder, "You don't have to come out. I can deal with it."

Sally, bless her, ignored him. "Anyone I know?" she asked, shuffling up behind him and resting a hand on his shoulder.

"What did you say your name is?" Harry asked me with each word sticking in his throat.

I told him.

He repeated it to Sally as if she were deaf, adding, "He was the kid evacuated to the Lockwoods in the war."

"That little boy with the fringe and the front teeth missing?" Sally laughed. "Well, what a funny old world this is. And he's brought his young lady to meet us. What are you doing, keeping them on the doorstep, Harry? Let them in, for God's sake, and let's all have a drink."

Harry decided not to make an issue of it. He

shrugged and stepped back, allowing Sally to shake our hands. I introduced Alice, using just her forename. I'm certain that Harry didn't recognize her. She was a small girl of eight when he'd last seen her.

I'd expected grandfather clocks and rosewood tables, but the drawing room we were shown into was furnished in steel, glass, and white leather. Only the marble fireplace and molded ceiling were antique. Sally, obviously used to people gaping, explained, "Everyone thinks we're puggoo-headed, filling a room like this with modern furniture, but Harry likes to get away from his business." *Puggoo-headed*. I was glad to hear a bit of Somerset. Once I would have filed it away in my memory for Duke, with "Or I, then?"

"You have a shop in Bath?" I asked.

"Nope," said Harry, making me wish I hadn't inquired.

Sally explained. "He has three warehouses. Two in Bristol, one in London."

"What do you drink?" Harry asked me.

He'd ignored Alice, so I turned to include her in the offer. She gave me a twitchy smile. She was extremely nervous. "Fruit juice would be fine, if you have one."

"Gallons," said Harry, as if it were someone's fault. "And yours?"

"A Scotch and soda."

He started to leave the room. Sally called, "Get me a vodka and . . ." She didn't finish because he'd ignored her. She waved us into chairs and offered us cigarettes, taking one herself and standing by the fireplace with a length of unstockinged leg protruding from the housecoat. "Harry's a big wheel in the antique world," she told us. "You're lucky to find him at home. He travels all over. Buys up the contents of houses and exports most of it to the States." Her eyes traveled to my shoes. "So you've had a day in the country."

I'd noticed the white carpet as we entered but failed to remember the state of our footwear. There were tracks to my chair.

Alice saw that I was literally wrong-footed and responded for me. "Yes, we went to see the farm where Theo stayed."

"You're American!" said Sally. "Harry will be delighted."

I couldn't imagine it. I pitched in again, taking the lead from Alice. "Yes, the farm hasn't changed much."

"Except for the orchards," commented Sally, drawing on her cigarette. "They grubbed out all the trees."

"Understandably," I said. "Frankly, I was surprised to find the Lockwoods still in occupation."

"Them? They're hard people," said Sally. "Did you speak to them?"

"Only Bernard, the son."

"He farms it all now, the main farm as well as Lower Gifford. The old couple look after the vegetables behind the house, and that's all."

"Do you keep up with them?"

She shook her head. "Barbara was a real pal, rest her soul, and her mother has been here for a coffee, but I've no time for the men."

"You visit the village sometimes?"

"Whenever I can. I know so many people there. Harry picks up a certain amount of business through the pub. He's never off duty." She fidgeted with the lapel of her housecoat. "I miss the old days."

"Like picking the apples?"

"Mm. The fun we had."

"Telling fortunes with apple pips."

She smiled at me. "Do you remember that?"

"Vividly. Barbara sliced the apple and got three pips. Tinker, tailor, soldier."

Sally's face changed. "And she split the soldier pip with the knife, poor love. She was terribly upset, being pregnant and everything."

"Did you know she was pregnant?"

"We had no secrets from each other. They were going to be married."

I said gently, "I'm afraid he already had a wife and child."

Sally shook her head. "That can't be true."

"Back in America."

There was an agonizing silence, ended by a creak of floorboards as Harry approached.

Sally snapped out in a small shocked voice, "You've got it all wrong." With an abrupt change of manner she turned, raised her voice, and addressed the open door. "We had a regular downpour here this afternoon, didn't we, Harry?"

He gave no answer. He seemed to ignore her most of the time.

I was in no shape to pick up the conversation. Sally's last comment had left me reeling. I wanted to ask more, but judging from her reaction to Harry, this wasn't the moment.

We were handed our drinks. Sally looked at hers and said, "What's this?"

"Grapefruit juice," said Harry without looking at her. "The ladies are drinking fruit juice."

"You're kidding!" said Sally, starting towards the door. "With vodka, maybe."

He grabbed her wrist in a surprisingly agile reflex and said, "Without."

She glared at him and said, "Prick." Then she tugged herself free and ran from the room.

Harry smugly called after her, "I locked it." He explained to us superfluously, "She isn't allowed alcohol."

An awkward silence ensued. The onus was on him to start a new line of conversation, and I didn't feel like helping.

It paid off. He said, "So you remember Duke?"

I nodded.

"Regular guy," said Harry. "Too bad."

I waited for more, and when it came, it was as sensational as anything Sally had said.

"He should be alive today."

"What do you mean?" demanded Alice in a

whisper. She was wound up to the snapping point.

"Just that, sweetheart. Duke was innocent. I could have saved him." Harry picked a cigar out of a ceramic pot on the mantelpiece and made us wait while he went through the ritual of lighting it.

Making it obvious that I'd need plenty of convincing, I commented, "You say you could have saved him but you didn't."

Harry glared at me through the smoke. "How could I? Where was I in 1945 when they put him on trial? Somewhere this side of Berlin, mopping up. I didn't see Duke after Normandy. Our units were separated after the landing. The first I heard of it was August '45, a piece of gossip over a beer. This padre from way back says to me, 'remember Duke Donovan, the tall New Yorker who wrote songs?' Did I know they took him back to England and hanged him for murder? Did I, hell!"

Skeptically, I said, "You think you should have been the star witness for the defense?"

"Am I getting through to you now?" said Harry, trading sarcasm.

Alice was hunched forward on the edge of the chair, pressing her whitened knuckles against her jaw. "How do you know that my daddy was innocent?"

So much for our ground rules, but who could have blamed her? The precise words she used weren't planned. She was so keyed up that the mention of her daddy was automatic.

151

Harry was on to it like a terrier. "Just who are you?"

Alice stared at him in a petrified silence. I doubt if she was capable of speech.

I answered for her. "She's the daughter of Duke and Eleanor Donovan."

He gave a quick, nervous laugh. "You don't say! Elly's child? This is Elly's child? Why didn't you tell me, for Christ's sake?"

I said truthfully, "We didn't know how you'd react."

He was busy adjusting, torn between anger and, I think, a residue of sentiment. "Can you beat that? I married her mother, did you know that? I'm her stepfather." He took a couple of steps towards Alice in recognition that some paternal gesture was wanted and actually put out a hand towards her shoulder without quite making contact. He let it down slowly and asked, "Tell me, is Elly still —"

I spoke for Alice again. "She died."

"No," said Harry with the awkwardness of an ex-husband with a nonexistent record of concern. "That's terrible. How?"

"A car crash earlier this year."

He rolled his eyes upwards. "Nobody told me."

I said unsparingly, "Is that surprising after you abandoned them?"

He turned away from me. "Alice, honey, if there's anything you need . . ."

She said without looking up, "Just tell me about my daddy."

Harry nodded, picked up his glass, and said, "First I need another drink. Anyone else?"

He left us alone.

I offered my Scotch and soda to Alice. "Want a sip of this?"

She shook her head.

I warned her, "Don't expect too much from Harry. He could be stringing us along."

I don't know if he heard my opinion, but he was back in the room a second after I'd given it, ready to go, like an actor on a second take. This time with more attack. "Okay, if you want to know the truth about your daddy, Alice, you picked the right guy. He and I were buddies from way back. We belonged to a boys' baseball club in Queens. Does that surprise you?" He mimed the pitcher's action. "And your mom used to come and watch. She was in high school with Duke. Eleanor Beech. Blonde like you and just as pretty. Well, almost. I could show you pictures."

I said acidly, "The words will do."

"Whatever you want. Elly Beech was Duke's girl, and I used to date her sometimes." He smiled at the memory. *"Date her?* I mean buy her an ice-cream soda at the drugstore and walk her home after. Duke was bigger than me, better-looking, a lean, dark Irish look that impressed girls." Harry paused to let us appreciate how golden-hearted he was, then added, "But I was a couple of years older. A man of the world. I could do voices and make her laugh. I may be

153

shorter than average, but I never had problems relating to women."

No, I thought, you never had problems, you bastard, but you gave your wives plenty.

Harry was on to his service career. He'd enlisted in December 1941, the day after America entered the war. "I was smart. The first volunteers took quick promotion. Inside eighteen months I was made up to sergeant. I told Duke, and he signed on as soon as he reached the age, in '42. He needed the pay to marry Elly, which he did, sometime in '43."

Alice supplied the date: "April fifth."

Harry flashed her a broad smile. "Thanks, sweetheart. You must be right, because they weren't married more than a couple of months before it was June and we were drafted to Shepton Mallet, England. Great name, crummy place. A stone cross, a prison, and five thousand GIs bored out of their skulls. Is it any wonder that I got reduced to the ranks for bringing girls onto the base at night?"

I couldn't trust myself to answer, so I said, "I've never been to Shepton Mallet."

"Don't bother," said Harry, and moved on. "So I was a private soldier, and naturally I linked up with my buddy, Duke. We'd borrow a jeep and go for rides. There was a lot of sympathy for me in the MT section."

"And Duke?" I put in quickly. "What was his standing?"

"A regular guy. Popular. Good musician.

Wrote his own songs. Anyone who could entertain us was made, believe me."

I nodded. "Barbara told me about the Columbus Day concert at the base. She was highly impressed with Duke's singing."

"Is that a fact? Yeah, I guess he could have made it as a songwriter. Country and western more than pop. He was working on a way of using the Somerset dialect in his songs. The way they talked down here amused him."

"I know. I used to collect words and phrases for him. He made lists."

Harry drew on his cigar and looked at me with a shade more respect. "That's right. He did. Matter of fact, Duke and his lists of words came in handy when I was dating Sally."

"You couldn't understand her?"

He pulled a face. "Christ, no, she wasn't a total hick. What I mean is, she was strictly brought up. Her parents didn't like her walking out with a GI, but a foursome was okay, so I persuaded Duke to make up the numbers with Barbara." He grinned complacently. "I told him it was a great way to get more Somerset words, and he bought it."

I grinned back. "Never."

"Straight up. I'm not kidding."

This simply didn't square with what I knew about Barbara. She'd walked up the lane almost every evening that autumn, telling her parents she was meeting Sally, when she was actually meeting Duke. She'd looked into my room sometimes at the end of an evening, flushed with love, her lips swollen from kissing. I *knew*, and I'd been punished for keeping her secret. I wouldn't have endured a beating from Mrs. Lockwood for nothing.

I told Harry, "Maybe he was kidding *you*."

Harry conceded a little. "Sure, he was doing me a favor. He was a great buddy."

I spelled it out for him. "Duke and Barbara were lovers."

I heard a sharp intake of breath from Alice.

Harry said, "No chance."

"For Christ's sake, she was expecting his child!"

Alice made a shrill, protesting cry. I avoided looking at her. I wanted this between Harry and me.

Harry slung his half-smoked cigar into the fireplace and stepped towards my chair, jowls quivery, red-faced with outrage. "Stand up and say that."

I replied through the fumes, "Read the post-mortem report. She was two months' pregnant."

He grabbed my sweater and tried to haul me upwards, but I gripped his forearm and resisted. My arms and shoulders are strong. I use them more than most people.

We might have stayed locked for some time if Alice hadn't snatched up my stick and jabbed it hard into Harry's ribs. He let go and staggered back, knocking over a glass-topped table and my drink as he went.

Alice was a revelation, eyes flashing behind

the gold frames. She told her stepfather, "Quit it, will you?"

Massaging his side, Harry said thickly, "He insulted my buddy."

Alice glared at him and said, "Loyalty isn't your strong suit, Harry." Then, to my surprise and extreme annoyance, she wheeled on me and said, "Quit bugging him with stupid crap like that. We came here to listen, not start a fight. This is *my* show, and I'm not letting anyone foul it up."

It was a kick in the teeth. All my animosity came surging back. For this headstrong, father-fixated girl I'd sacrificed my weekend, missing my sleep, seen off the press, driven all the way to Somerset, faced a hostile farmer with a shotgun, and ruined a set of clothes.

I could have pointed out that if I'd left her to do the talking, we'd still be standing on the doorstep.

Instead I controlled my anger. I gave her the look of a man who has run through his fund of sympathy. "Your show? Run it the way you want."

Let's give her credit: She didn't falter. The flurry of action had taken the edge off her nerves. She tossed her hair back from her forehead, tucked the walking stick under her arm like a drill sergeant, and told Harry, "Pick up the table."

He obeyed without a murmur.

FOURTEEN

"Why don't you sit down?" When her suggestion had been acted on, Alice gave Harry a cool,
unfilial look. "You said you could have put the
court right on a few things. This is your chance.
I'm going to take you through the crucial days
of 1943."

With an air of authority that wouldn't have
disgraced a learned counsel examining a witness, she drew Harry's story from him: how he
and Duke had met me in Mrs. Mumford's and
driven out to Gifford Farm; how they'd met
Barbara and offered to help gather the apples.

"Why?" asked Alice.

Harry's eyebrows lifted, but he gave no answer. All the bounce had gone out of him.

"Why did you offer to help?"

"Two bored GIs looking for free drinks and
friendship, I guess."

"So, was Barbara the attraction?"

"Sure, she was pretty. She had the whitest
skin you ever saw. Rosy cheeks. Fine black hair.
She was a sweet kid but kind of remote." To this
touching eulogy he added the footnote, "I
didn't expect to score with her."

158

"Did Duke?" asked Alice. If proof were wanted of her self-control, it was here in the way she put the question, as if the daddy she'd never mentioned before without a tremor in her voice was suddenly a cipher.

Harry shook his head. "He was a married man."

"So were hundreds of other GIs who went with English girls," said Alice. "You can be frank with me."

"All the time he was over here, Duke never looked at a woman."

She said in the same reasonable tone, "That's not true, is it? He escorted Barbara to the Columbus Day concert."

None of Alice's composure rubbed off on Harry. His voice rose to a protesting squeak. "He did it to help me out." Then his words came in a rush. "This was twenty years ago. Nice girls moved in pairs, safety in numbers from studs like me, understand? I couldn't date Sally without finding someone for her friend. So Duke came along. He drove the jeep, hands on the wheel, Barbara beside him clutching her handbag. They didn't even talk much. All the action happened in the rear seat."

"And after that evening?"

Harry looked vacant.

"Didn't they meet secretly?" Alice asked.

"Where was this, for God's sake?"

"In the lanes around the farm. Barbara would

go for evening walks. Duke would be waiting with the jeep."

"Sweetheart, who gave you this crap?"

Alice didn't answer. She didn't even look in my direction. Harry said, "Listen, Duke spent most evenings writing to Elly. Take it from me, if he'd been going out nights in the jeep, I'd have known. Jesus, I'd have been with him."

"Maybe he didn't tell you."

"Nuts."

Still unruffled, Alice said, "Let's backtrack, shall we? You did some shooting on the farm with Mr. Lockwood and his son?"

Harry nodded. "Joke. The only gun we could lay our hands on was a .45. That's a pistol, an automatic. We shot nothing. And before you ask, Barbara wasn't in the party."

"But on another occasion you took her with you."

"That was different. Duke had promised to give the boy a turn with the .45." Harry's eyes fastened on me. "Am I right?"

I confirmed it.

He continued, "Barbara just tagged along, as I recall. We took a few shots at an oilcan."

"And afterwards?"

"We put the gun in the hallstand where old Lockwood kept his shotguns." He gave a sly grin. "That .45 was like a bottle of Coke — non-returnable."

"So anyone could have taken it from there on the day of the murder?"

Harry passed no comment.

Alice moved on. "Let's come to the cider pressing. While it was going on, you and Duke drove out to the farm several times, didn't you?"

"Sure."

"You watched Mr. Lockwood put mutton in the casks?"

"Yup."

"And you heard Bernard mention that he'd spotted Cliff Morton's bicycle in a ditch on the farm?"

Harry's response was more assertive this time. He wagged a fat finger in the air. "That's another thing. Duke hardly met the guy he's supposed to have shot. The first time we came to pick apples — this is back in September — there was some kind of incident. I believe Morton was caught trying it on with Barbara. He was given the bum's rush. We didn't see him again."

At this point in the exchange I interrupted. Harry was so wide of the mark that I couldn't prevent myself. I said, "Whether Duke knew the man is immaterial. The motive wasn't jealousy. He killed him because of the savage attack he made on Barbara."

I was rewarded with a cold stare from Alice. "Will you let me continue?" she asked in a tone that left no doubt that she would. She returned to Harry. "On that afternoon you drove out to the farm with Duke to invite the girls to a party."

"Thanksgiving Day," Harry confirmed. "And

before you ask, I was the organizer. I had it down as my benefit night. You may not believe this after what you saw just now, but Sal was hot for me in those days. I knew I was ready to score. All I had to do was set it up, keep the Shoesmith family sweet. So I talked Duke into being Barbara's escort again. I really had to sell it to him, I can tell you. Finally, the songwriting swung it my way. He was composing these songs in the Somerset dialect, using the words he'd heard. They were three-quarters written, but he was stuck for a few more lines."

"Which you told him Barbara could provide?"

"You got it."

"You're quite certain that there was nothing between them?"

"Duke and Barbara? Zilch."

"On both sides? I mean, how about Barbara? Did she have romantic ideas about Duke?"

"I doubt it. If you ask me, she was doing Sally a favor."

Alice said thoughtfully, "Maybe I should ask Sally."

"Sure. Why not?" Harry was all for the spotlight moving to someone else.

"Let's finish this. I believe you called for Sally on the way to the farm."

"Correct."

"And?"

Resignedly, he wound himself up again. "The party was a surprise. She'd never heard of Thanksgiving, but she was over the moon when

I invited her. I told her we'd pick up Barbara on the way. She put on some face and a pretty dress and we were on the road inside the hour."

"And when you got to Gifford Farm?"

Harry took off his glasses and wiped them, remembering. "There was a holiday atmosphere, not for Thanksgiving but for the cider pressing. They were on the last load of apples, and the machine was going like a steam hammer. Old man Lockwood had treated everyone to extra cider and given the farmhands an early finish. Mrs. Lockwood was offering hot scones and cream, but we wanted to ask Barbara to the party first, so she could get ready."

"You told the Lockwoods about the party?"

"No need. We had Sally with us in a pink chiffon dress."

"She must have been cold."

"Sitting on my lap? You're kidding. To answer your question, we told them about the party and they raised no objection, so Duke and I went off to find Barbara. She should be milking, they told us. She wasn't. She hadn't been. The cows were still waiting with their udders straining. We went back to see if anyone had a better idea. No dice." Harry stopped and jerked his head in my direction. "He can tell you the rest."

Alice wasn't letting him off. "I've had his account," she told Harry in a firm, no-nonsense voice. "I came here for yours."

"The works?"

"All of it. Everything."

"You're going to be disappointed," he warned her.

"Try me," said Alice.

Hearing all this, I was veering between anger and admiration. She'd handled Harry brilliantly, keeping control without seeming to antagonize him. Her grasp of the disjointed and highly subjective story I'd unfolded the previous evening was rock-sure. What's more, she'd sorted it into its proper sequence. She'd match any computer in processing information. Believe me, I was smarting from the rebukes she'd dealt me, and peeved that she didn't challenge some of Harry's wrongheaded assertions, yet I'm forced to admit that she got more from him than I would have done.

And for all his denials, some of the most interesting details came at the end.

"I was just a bystander," he insisted. "I heard about the rape from Sally, and she got it from Mrs. Lockwood."

"Aren't we jumping forward here?" said Alice. "You left us with the cows not milked and no sign of Barbara."

Harry put back his glasses and blinked in a puzzled way. "But you know what happened. The boy found Cliff Morton in the act of raping Barbara and ran out to tell the first person he saw, who was Duke."

"No," said Alice serenely. "I'm not asking that. I want to know what *you* were doing."

Silence.

He shifted in his chair. "Well, I, em . . . I joined in the search."

"Where did you search?"

"The cowsheds. Took me some time. All those stalls."

"And, of course, you found nothing. Did you hear anything?"

Harry considered the question. "The cider mill was still grinding."

"So you heard that. Anything else?"

"No."

"You searched the cowshed, and then?"

"Back to the house."

"You crossed the yard, then?"

"Sure."

"See anyone?"

"Barbara, with her mother. They were ahead of me, moving towards the kitchen door. Great, I thought, we found her. All we need now is Duke, so he can invite her to the party. I was about to go find him when I sensed something wrong. I took another look at the two women. I just had a back view of them, and they were almost through the door by this time. Mrs. Lockwood had her hands on Barbara's shoulders . . . like this. Barbara's hair was loose, and her head was right back and shaking, like she was hysterical."

"Screaming?"

Harry shrugged. "The damn machine was still going. Far as I could tell, Mrs. Lockwood was holding her upright. They went inside. I'm standing there scratching my head when out comes Sally."

"From the kitchen?"

"Yeah. She runs over to me and tells me Barbara was attacked. I ask her who did it and she doesn't know. She's pretty upset herself, and she asks me to take her home. I ask her where Duke is. She shakes her head and tries to pull me towards the jeep. She says leave him. Just take me home. I'm telling her I can't do that when Duke comes around the side of the cider house and says let's go. He gets in the jeep and starts up."

"How was he looking?" asked Alice.

"Kind of solemn. Tight-lipped."

"His appearance. Blood on his clothes? Any sign of violence?"

"Not that I saw."

"He was in uniform, I expect?"

"Sure."

"Blouse and pants? The buttons all fixed as usual?"

"I guess I'd have noticed if not."

"And how was his behavior?"

"A little erratic," Harry admitted. "That's how it seemed at the time. I asked if he knew what happened to Barbara. He said, as if he knew all about it, there's nothing we can do. I said for Christ's sake, Duke, there's plenty we can do. For a start, we can find the creep who attacked her. Duke said leave it. He told me to get in the jeep. He spoke with a kind of au-

166

thority. Sally was already aboard, yelling at me to get in for God's sake. So I did."

Alice had listened in rapt concentration. She was standing with her two hands on my stick, holding it forward like a divining rod. "I want to get this straight," she told Harry. "Were these Duke's exact words: 'There's nothing we can do. Leave it. Get in the jeep'?"

"Jeez, it was a long time ago," pleaded Harry.

"Think."

"I'm ninety percent sure. He may have thrown in a stronger word."

"But the rest stands?"

"Sure."

She paused for thought, staring up at the stuccoed ceiling. Presently she nodded at Harry. "And then?"

"We drove off."

"Where to?"

Harry's face showed the strain as he wrestled with a memory. A new set of creases branched out from his eyes and mouth. "I told you Duke was at the wheel. At the crossroads he turned in the Shepton Mallet direction and put his foot on the gas. He didn't give a thought to Sally. She was in the backseat with me. She says to me where the heck are we going? I can't go to the party after what happened to my friend. So I stuck my hand on Duke's shoulder and asked him to stop."

"And did he?"

"Not before we were halfway to Shepton

Mallet, and then he refused to turn the jeep."

"Why?"

Harry sighed. "How do I know? I can't say what had gotten into him. He started giving me the needle. He said what's with you two? You got it made. You don't really need Barbara or me to have a good time. Make hay. Have a ball."

"Couldn't he see that Sally was upset?"

"I just couldn't get through to him."

"Could Sally?"

"Sal? She was too scared to speak. She had rape on her mind, I guess."

"So what happened?"

"When it was obvious we were at a stalemate, he told me to take over the jeep. I could drive Sally home if I wanted, but not with him on board. He'd rather walk to Shepton Mallet."

Alice's eyes widened. "And did he?"

Harry gave a nod. "Wasn't much over three miles. I turned the jeep and drove Sally home. End of story."

Alice preferred to reach her own conclusion. "Was it really the end? Didn't you see Duke again that evening?"

"If I had, we wouldn't have spoken."

"What time did you get back?"

"I couldn't say. I had a beer in the Jolly Gardener, and then I drove around for a while, looking for a pickup. Just wasn't my night."

"Was this before midnight?" Alice persisted.

"Yeah."

"And was anything said when you saw Duke next?"

"About what happened? Nothing. Frost."

"You fell out?"

"That's the size of it. We didn't speak for weeks."

"Not even after Barbara committed suicide?"

"Not even then. Much later, after we'd both been posted to Colchester, I mentioned it. Duke knew about Barbara. He said it was really sad."

"Nothing else?"

"Nothing. It was a sensitive topic."

"I understand," said Alice in a way that signaled a respite for Harry. She picked her fruit juice off the table and took a sip.

Remarkably, considering how drained he looked, Harry was unwilling to leave it at that. He appeared to sense that some self-justifying statement was still necessary. After he'd taken out a colored handkerchief and wiped his brow, he added, "You know, when I first heard about the murder, and Duke taking the rap, I didn't believe it. I can't describe the feeling. Coming on top of the war, which to a GI was totally unreal until you got in the firing line, it was way over my head. Took me weeks to come to terms with it — I mean, just accepting that Duke had been hanged. He was no killer."

Harry stopped to blow his nose. He was visibly affected by what he'd been saying. He resumed. "Finally I read a book on the case, *The Somerset Skull*, by some English journalist."

"Barrington Miller," I said with contempt. "A real scissors-and-paste job."

"True," said Harry, "but it had the essential facts on the trial, and it told me the prosecution was garbage. Sexual jealousy? No chance. He never had sex with the girl. If she was pregnant, believe me, it was some other guy. I told you how it was between Duke and Barbara."

" 'Zilch,' I think, was how you described it," I said, observing neutrality. Alice was silent, drawing breath, perhaps, for a heart-to-heart with Sally.

"Take that U.S. Army major in court to speak for Duke's character," Harry said with a sharp note of censure. "It was character assassination. They couldn't get over the fact that he heisted a .45 and used a jeep for private trips. They didn't say he was a loyal husband, one of the gentlest, most civilized soldiers in the army." He stopped to wipe his nose again. "I'm sorry. You don't want to hear all this. I just want to explain my position. After reading all this crap I had to decide what to do about it. I was back in the States by this time. What could I do to put the injustice right? Send a letter to the London *Times*? Write to the Lord Chief Justice? Whatever I did, I couldn't bring Duke back to life. Alice, honey, do you know what I did?"

"Found my mother," said Alice flatly.

"Precisely. Help the living. Elly was in a pitiful state. No job, no pension, and a child to raise. And bitterly ashamed of what Duke had done. I put her right on that for a start. Then I married her. I won't say it was much of a marriage, but I got her through a bad time. We came to an understanding about Duke — not to make waves, not to write to *The Times*, not even to mention him. You know why? For your sake, sweetheart. I respected your mother's wishes." With that off his chest Harry got to his feet and said, "Whose glass is empty?"

Alice had listened impassively. Now she brushed aside Harry's diversionary gesture. "If it's all the same to you, we'd like to meet your wife again."

"No problem," claimed Harry. He fairly scuttled through the door.

Alice handed me back my stick. "I have a feeling that Mrs. Ashenfelter II might respond better to you."

But as it turned out, Sally was in no shape to respond to anyone. Harry came back grim-faced and announced, "No dice. Sally's out cold. She took a chisel to the cocktail cabinet, and she's been through a bottle and a half of vodka."

FIFTEEN

We wanted to eat. A straightforward matter? Not in Bath on a Sunday evening in October 1964. All the restaurants were dark, and the hotels didn't want to know us. "Sorry, residents only" should be translated into Latin and incorporated in the city's coat of arms. We finally gained grudging admittance to a dingy basement in Great Pulteney Street that doubled as the dining room and lounge of a small private hotel called the Annual Cure. Top marks for local color, but not, I think, for attracting customers. We were the only diners.

Alice was still brooding on our visit to the Ashenfelters, so I picked up the gravy-stained menu. It was written without much regard to spelling.

"If you fancy something out of the ordinary, I see they serve *farmhouse girll*," I commented too loudly, because the manager was standing unseen at my shoulder.

"You don't like?" he asked. "You go somewhere else." I believe he was mid-European.

I pointed out the error, wishing I hadn't spoken.

He snatched the menu from me, penciled in a correction, pushed it back, and said with acid, "Schoolteacher?"

"Something like that."

We both settled on plaice and french flies without going into the orthography. Alice asked for the rest room, the ladies', and the lavatory before she was understood and directed upstairs.

As she pushed back her chair I murmured something about a search party but failed to amuse her. Mentally, she hadn't caught up yet. I doubt whether our shabby surroundings had made any impression on her at all.

Alone at the table, I made my own review of the day's discoveries. No doubt Alice would snap out of her introspection soon and start an earnest discussion. I wanted my thoughts in trim.

Two observations on Alice.

First, she was dangerous to be with. She might easily have got us shot by blurting out her identity to Bernard Lockwood. She'd treated Harry, another violent character, with reckless disrespect.

Second, on the credit side, she'd got results. Thanks to her open approach, we'd traced Harry and identified him as her stepfather. We'd learned of his marriage to Sally Shoesmith. And we'd been given a different slant on the relationship between Duke and Barbara: According to Harry, they weren't lovers, after all. The fact that I knew this to be untrue didn't detract from its significance. Harry was either deluded or a villain.

But we're dealing with Alice. I wasn't blind to her motives. Any female who could slip so rapidly out of a little-girl-lost role and into bed wasn't dewy-eyed. She'd used me, manipulated me, played on my reactions. As it happened, I didn't particularly mind, because through the bewildering shifts of character I'd perceived a personality I liked. She was intelligent, resilient, sometimes wrongheaded, but brave, unusually brave. Different.

I've told you about the moment when I was toweling Alice's hair in front of the fire in the pub and I knew that I wanted her. To be brutally honest — and haven't I kept faith with you up to now? — the wanting was all on my side. I'd picked up no signals from Alice.

Well, almost none. If there had been a moment of mutual closeness, it was earlier. Smile if you wish, but I don't mean when we were in bed together. That was an experience, a turn-on, as exciting as anything my body had been privileged to share in but exclusively sensual.

I'm talking about another moment. Remember when we stepped over the puddles at Gifford Farm and she took my hand? And slipped her arm about my waist in the hayloft? Then, I believe, other possibilities beckoned us, like understanding, respect, and maybe even affection.

Yet what happened on the drive to Bath when

I tried to kiss her? What brought on the frost?

I traced it back to our conversation in the hayloft. I'd balked at some of the intimate questions she'd fired at me concerning Cliff Morton's attack on Barbara. I mean, I didn't duck out. I'd simply felt uncomfortable and shown it. I'd appeared evasive.

So if I wanted Alice, there were bridges to be mended. I needed to be constructive about what we'd seen and heard.

For a start, our trip to Gifford Farm. Bernard couldn't have made it more plain that he was troubled to find us at the farm. *What's past is over* was his attitude, and I had some sympathy for it. I'd felt the same until Alice had forced my hand. But I hadn't seen her off with a shotgun.

I could understand Bernard and his parents wanting to forget. They'd been through hell since Barbara's rape and suicide. The inquest. The discovery of the skull in the cask and the ruin of their cider business. The police swarming over their farm digging for human remains. The suspicions that George Lockwood had shot Morton. Nor had it ended with Duke's arrest. They'd all been called to testify at the trial.

A niggling thought intruded here. In their understandable wish to get a positive verdict, and the whole thing forgotten as soon as possible, might the Lockwoods have overstated the evidence against Duke? The prosecution had been mounted largely on forensic testimony, backed by circumstantial evidence from the Lockwoods and myself. We, between us, had provided the picture of Duke as the vengeful lover. I'm not saying that the Lockwoods were guilty of perjury, and I certainly didn't go along with everything Harry had told us, but could they have misinterpreted some of Barbara's actions?

Which brought me to Harry.

His version of events was sensational. Maybe *fantastic* is a better word. By his account Duke had no regard for Barbara whatsoever. He'd had to be persuaded, if not press-ganged, into partnering her. According to Harry, those romantic evening walks in the Somerset lanes simply hadn't included Duke. On the afternoon of the rape and murder, Duke had appeared disenchanted, but hardly like a man who had just blown out another's brains.

Why, I wondered, had Harry suggested such things if they weren't true?

There was a clue. It was his revelation that he and Duke had been boyhood friends, rivals for Alice's mother, Elly. Harry had treated it lightly. Easy now to dismiss it as casual dates with ice-cream sodas. How had he felt at the time, when Duke had cut him out and married Elly? No bitterness? No festering resentment?

If there was none, and it was nothing to him, why had he married Elly himself when the opportunity came?

Suppose Harry, Duke's so-called buddy, cynically and deliberately took advantage of their time away from home to promote and encourage an affair between Duke and the first available girl. Suppose it was always Harry's plan to disclose to Elly that her young husband was unfaithful. Simple, really, to work on a man's loneliness: "Just make up a foursome, Duke, so I can get some time with Sally." And to Sally: "You know, my buddy is incredibly shy, but he really fancies your friend Barbara." A few encouraging signals from Barbara and the fuse was lit.

Then suppose the whole scheme misfired because of Cliff Morton's attack on Barbara. Duke killed Morton out of some rash notion of honor, and Barbara committed suicide in shame and despair. Harry was shocked, no doubt. But being an opportunist, he waited for the dust to settle. Then he saw his chance. When the law had taken its course, he went to visit poor, widowed Elly as her caring friend.

As an explanation, it fitted the personalities as well as the known facts. It accounted for Harry's coolness to Alice and me when we arrived on his doorstep wanting to discuss the murder. His first instinct had been to send us away, his second to deny that there was ever anything serious between Duke and Barbara.

It was thanks to Sally that we'd got inside.

So what about Sally?

If there was any truth in my theory, she must have been involved. Yet she'd come to our aid, invited us in when Harry would have shut the door. Clearly there was tension between Harry and her, most apparent when he'd gone out of the room to collect the drinks and she'd been on the point of telling us something about Duke's relationship with Barbara. What had Sally said when we talked about the fortune-telling game with the apple, when Barbara cut through the last pip — the "soldier pip"? "She was terribly upset, being pregnant and everything . . . We had no secrets from each other. They were going to be married." And when I'd gently pointed out to Sally that Duke already had a wife and child in America, she'd appeared not to know about it, and said, "You've got it all wrong." Poor Sally. Hadn't Harry ever told her the truth?

I'd have liked another word with Sally.

I didn't get any further before Alice reappeared. Rather to my disappointment, she'd refastened her plait. She looked more solemn than ever. And, uniquely in my experience of women, she hadn't taken the opportunity in the ladies' to touch up her lipstick. Not much encouragement there. I prepared for the worst, and it wasn't long in coming.

She studied me for a while, as if she'd made up her mind that something had to be resolved between us, and finally said, "I'm staying here tonight. I've booked a single room upstairs."

I said inanely, "What?"

She waited for it to sink in.

Meanwhile I was eyeing the stack of ketchup bottles on the shelf, each with its red deposit caked around the cap. Anyone who contemplated a night in this place had to be desperate.

"Why, for God's sake? It's a hole."

"I can see that."

"Is it me? Something I said to upset you?"

"No particular thing."

"What, then?"

The food arrived, dried-up fish and undercooked chips without vegetables or garnish, slammed in front of us, followed by one of the ketchup bottles.

I said with all the consideration I could muster, "Alice, I'd like to know what this is about."

She tightened her mouth and said nothing.

I told her, "I'm not going to leave you in a dump like this without a very good explanation."

She pushed her plate aside. She hadn't touched the food. I said across the chasm that had opened between us, "Don't you think I'm entitled to be told?"

Something disturbingly akin to contempt flickered across her face.

I wasn't giving up. "This relates to something you asked me earlier, doesn't it?"

A response at last. She nodded.

I said, "About what happened in the hayloft?"

She mouthed the word *yes*.

So we were back to the rape.

She must have seen the muscles tighten along my jawline. She gave me a warning look, narrowing her eyes.

I said, "Has something prompted this?"

"Sure. What we just heard from Harry."

"Harry? He was lying through his teeth."

After an interval to sharpen up the sarcasm she asked, "How did you get to be such an infallible judge of character, Theo? Is it intuition, sixth sense, or just refusing ever to trust a Yank?"

I smiled ironically. "Harry?"

"Not only Harry. My daddy too."

"I trusted him."

"Not when he said things you didn't want to believe."

"Such as?"

"The way he really felt about Barbara. There was never anything serious between them."

I frowned. "He said that?"

"In court. On oath."

"He was confused."

"Theo, it's on record. I read it in one of your books. There was nothing serious. He said it."

I commented offhandedly, "Depends what you mean by serious. I'd say her condition indicated something serious."

She scraped back her chair and said witheringly, "Is this the garbage you were trying to peddle to Harry? Are you seriously suggesting my daddy got her pregnant?"

She had every right to feel defensive about Duke. I loved him, too, and the truth hurt. "Someone did, Alice. She wasn't promiscuous."

"I'm not questioning that. I question the assumption that my daddy was responsible."

I leaned back in my chair. "Who do you think was the father, then?"

"Cliff Morton. You told me it was him."

"I told you what the gossip was in 1943." I leaned forward. "She was two months' pregnant when she died at the end of November. She'd been going out with Duke since September."

Alice clicked her tongue and looked away, as if it were futile listening to me.

I took a mouthful of the pale chips and chewed them, letting her brood on what I'd said. After an interval I said, "I expect you're thinking of the incident in the apple orchard, when Morton was given his marching orders. You think he may have made her pregnant then? It's true that she was pretty upset and so were the Lockwoods. She had love bites on her neck and shoulders. But as for full sex, no, that doesn't fit the facts. They would have treated it more seriously. Everyone would have. I had the impression there was some grappling in the long grass, a few snatched kisses, not much more."

"With Barbara's consent?"

I felt my blood run cold. "Of course not."

Alice's eyebrows jutted above the level of her glasses. "Why not?"

She was either incredibly wide of the mark or trying to goad me. Deciding to treat it lightly, I gave a laugh that was exhaled more than voiced. "She despised the man. He had a bad reputation. No regular work. He dodged the call-up. The entire family despised him."

181

"They employed him to pick apples."

"Force of circumstance. Men were in short supply."

She felt for her plait and traced one of the strands with her fingertip.

I said, "You won't make me believe that Barbara allowed Cliff Morton to . . . to . . ."

"You can't even bring yourself to mention it, can you?" said Alice in a voice that mingled pity and contempt. "Theo, you idolized that girl. She was sweet to you, and you turned her into a saint. I don't blame you. I had crushes on people myself when I was a kid. Only you're not a nine-year-old boy anymore. For God's sake let's talk about this in an adult fashion, because I think you're way off-beam over Barbara. I think she loved Cliff Morton."

"Impossible."

"Will you let me finish? Let's start with some facts of life. Simple mathematics. Barbara was found to be two months' pregnant at the time of her death, right? When precisely did she kill herself?"

"On the Sunday. November thirtieth."

"So she conceived in late September or very early the following month."

"Presumably."

"And it was late September when my daddy first came to the farm."

"True." At least there were some facts we could agree on. I took a fish bone from my mouth and parked it at the edge of my plate. I had a glimmer of where this was leading but only a glimmer. A man isn't so habituated to counting weeks and months.

She added, "If I got it right from you, they didn't spend any time together until the Columbus Day concert."

She'd fanned the glimmer into a spark.

"Columbus Day is October twelfth. These days we observe it on the second Monday in the month, but in the war it was always the same." She watched me without emotion as she repeated, "October twelfth, Theo."

I stared at her blankly. Why hadn't I worked it out for myself? I took a deep breath and admitted with as much dignity as I could salvage, "Duke couldn't have been the father of her child."

"Thank you." She looked over her glasses. "But somebody must have been."

I said with loathing, "That bastard Morton. He *did* rape her in the apple orchard."

Pointedly, she commented, "You told me just now it doesn't fit the facts."

"It has to," I blustered. "I was mistaken."

"No," said Alice. "You were right. You're not going to like this, Theo, but Barbara and Cliff were sweethearts." She put up a restraining hand. "Before you hit the roof, will you answer me this? When was the first time you noticed Cliff?"

"That morning in the orchard, I suppose."

"Would you try to recall it precisely, please?"

I gave a sharp sigh of impatience. The way she was addressing me was strikingly reminiscent of the cross-examination she'd made of Harry Ashenfelter. Well, if she wanted me on the witness stand, she'd find that I had a poor regard for her latest theory. I reminded her coolly, "I think I told you this before. It was during the break when Mrs. Lockwood brought out the tea. Quite a few of the people there were strangers to me, but I noticed Morton because he collected a mug of tea for Barbara and sat beside her. It proves nothing."

"You were just a little put out because it cut across your plans as a matchmaker. That's why you noticed him, isn't that so?"

I wasn't letting that pass unchallenged. "A matchmaker, no. I never actively promoted the friendship between Duke and Barbara."

She rephrased it. "They were both special people in your eyes, and you hoped they would link up."

I accepted that.

Alice said, "Let's move on to that afternoon. If I understood you right, Barbara quietly went missing in some remote part of the orchard."

"*Quietly?*" I objected. "That puts a whole different emphasis on what happened, as if it were furtive."

"Was she dragged screaming into the woods, then?"

"Well, no, but . . ."

"And you heard no screams later? Isn't it possible that she slipped away of her own volition to meet Cliff?"

"Possible," I conceded, making it plain that the possibility was extremely remote.

She was undeterred. "You're pretty sure the Lockwoods didn't like Cliff?"

"On the couple of occasions he was mentioned, they spoke disparagingly of him."

"So if Barbara took a shine to him, they wouldn't have been over the moon about it?"

I frowned. "What are you getting at?"

"A plausible explanation of what happened that afternoon. Correct me if I'm wrong, but isn't this how you described it? Mrs. Lockwood noticed Barbara was missing in the tea break and sent her husband to the other side of the orchard to look for her. Some time after, Cliff emerged from there and marched off — sorry, cycled off — into the sunset without speaking to anyone. Then you saw Barbara in tears and with her hair unfastened, coming from the same direction, with her father following. She ran right past her mother to the farmhouse." Alice paused. "Wouldn't you agree that Barbara's behavior was more indicative of someone caught out than someone who was the victim of an attack?"

I was unable to reply. As Alice had pointed out, I'd said myself that rape didn't fit the facts. Her explanation did — if you could swallow the grotesque suggestion that Morton was Barbara's lover.

The manager came back to collect our plates and see if we wanted the peach melba. We opted for coffee. I needed that moment's distraction.

"Out of a bottle, no doubt," I remarked to Alice.

She nodded automatically, impatient to press on. Her eyes were dilated — I suppose with the excitement of defending her daddy. "Now let's talk about that remark of Sally's that we'd got it all wrong about Barbara and the apple pip. Sally was Barbara's closest friend, yes?"

"Yes."

"So if anyone knew about Barbara's love life, it was Sally. If I understand it right about the business with the apple, the girls believed that the number of pips would tell them what kind of man they would marry. Now, when Barbara cut the apple in half, she got two pips: tinker, tailor. She cut one of the halves and got no more pips, so she cut the second half and found one: soldier. Will you listen, Theo? The soldier pip was severed and Barbara was pretty upset, because it was a bad omen. I think you said someone actually saw her crying in the afternoon."

"It's understandable," I said. "They take their superstitions seriously in Somerset. Strangely enough, it could have been a premonition of tragedy if you believe that Duke was already a doomed man."

"Not Duke," said Alice.

I stared at her without understanding.

She said, "Cliff Morton."

I gaped.

She said, "Cliff was the doomed man."

I shook my head. "Duke was the soldier."

"Not the one Barbara had in mind. Cliff had just received his call-up papers. She was thinking of him. She was about to lose him to the draft. Her lover. And when the apple pip was cut, she took it as a sign that he'd be killed in combat. Don't you see, Theo? She wouldn't shed tears over my daddy. She hardly knew him yet."

I couldn't fault her logic. If you assumed a relationship between Barbara and Cliff, it *was* a convincing explanation. Looking down, I found that I'd torn the plastic tablecloth.

"Do you see now why Sally told us we got it all wrong?" said Alice to underline the point.

"All right," I said, switching to the offensive, "but if Barbara was so attached to Morton, how do you account for her going to the concert with Duke?"

"Bluff. She used it as a decoy, to reassure her parents. They disapproved of Cliff. They may even have banned her from seeing him after the incident in the orchard. So she pretended she was taking up with one of the GIs."

I had her now. She had a good brain, and up to this point she'd concocted a plausible version of events, but I knew she was wrong over this.

I said with mild irony, "Pretended?"

"That's right, Theo. Like Harry said, there

was never anything serious between them."

"Barbara didn't confide in Harry. She confided in me. That evening you were talking about, her first evening out with Duke, she came to my room afterwards and talked to me about it."

She sighed and looked at her fingernails. "You told me."

I wasn't having it brushed aside. "She was radiant with excitement."

"Okay, she had a good time at the concert. I figure a girl didn't get much entertainment in wartime."

I said in the hectoring voice I sometimes used with difficult students, "Alice, I've done you the courtesy of listening to you. Now you can do likewise. She wasn't simply talking about the concert. She confided her thoughts about Duke. She said she was bursting with pride when he went on the stage to sing. She liked him: the way he treated her, his quiet manner, so different from the expectation she had of an American soldier. He was shy but with a gentle sense of humor. She told me she'd be seeing him again."

"She was using you," said Alice tersely.

"Come off it, that's unfair."

"She wanted her parents to get the idea she'd transferred her interest to my daddy, so she fed you this slush."

I shook my head. "You're wrong. She used to go out every evening to meet him."

"Do you know that for certain? Did you see them together? Ever? She was meeting Cliff."

She grasped her plait and flicked it behind her shoulder. "And before you tell me about Mrs. Lockwood spanking you, has it crossed your mind that she *wanted* to be told that Barbara was seeing a GI and not the local good-for-nothing? Think about that, Theo."

I did. Like so much else she'd said, it outraged me by challenging a version of events I'd grown up with and drawn comfort from, yet it had a sickening plausibility. I found myself remembering the eruption of strong language the morning in the cider house when Bernard Lockwood told his parents he'd noticed Morton's bicycle on the farm. I'd been shocked by the force of their reaction.

Two chipped cups were put in front of us, each containing clear, tepid water with a teaspoon anchored in something brown and glutinous. Stirring made no appreciable difference. We were too preoccupied to complain.

We had different ideas of what lay ahead. Up to now Alice had made all the running. This theory that had seemed a rank outsider at the start had cleared each fence and was still looking strong. I was sure there was one barrier it couldn't surmount.

After a period of silence I said, broaching it with caution, "You know, if someone wanted to choose between your interpretation and mine, they might be in two minds, except for one thing: There's no getting around the fact that Morton raped Barbara."

Her eyes behind the glasses were like chips of flint. She didn't speak a syllable.

I added less guardedly, "It makes nonsense of everything you've said up to now."

She found her voice and pitched it low, with an undertone of scorn. "Whose word have we got that this rape ever took place? Yours alone."

So that's your response, I thought. A straight challenge. I said, "It was accepted by a judge and jury. Are you putting yourself above them?"

She answered stiffly, "The judge and jury were appointed to hear a case of murder, not rape. The story of the rape was never seriously questioned. No medical evidence was given. They took the word of a nine-year-old boy."

I said, "I may have been nine then, but I'm twenty-nine now, and that was rape."

Alice smiled faintly, not a friendly smile. "This afternoon I got you to describe minutely what you saw that afternoon in the hayloft. The way they were lying, the sounds they made, the movements. I'm not the world's expert on sex, but I figure I know more about what a woman feels than you, because nothing in what you described to me was untypical of passionate love-making. You said she had her clothes rucked up. She was gasping and crying out, turning her head, squirming. Do you know what it's like for a woman to experience a powerful orgasm, or haven't you noticed?"

I said, "Oh, come on. She was beating her fists on the floor."

Alice took a quick, impatient breath. "Theo, she'd have been trying to push him away if he was raping her."

She was looking at me through the glasses, entreating me to make some concession to her theory. I was intractable.

She persisted. "As a child, it's understandable that a sight of adults in the act of love would alarm you, but surely with maturity you can analyze what you witnessed?"

I was in no frame of mind to analyze anything. I didn't need to listen to her interpretation. I'd been there when it happened.

Angered by my lack of reaction, she pushed her face closer, taunting me. "Tell me this, then. Why was Cliff on the farm at all if it wasn't at Barbara's invitation?"

I didn't respond.

She loosed off a salvo of questions. "Why did Barbara go up to the hayloft? And when my daddy ran into the barn, why didn't he pull them apart?"

"The attack was over," I couldn't resist pointing out. "He went for the gun."

Her face tightened into an expression that I hadn't seen before, a hard, accusing stare. "That isn't true, is it? He had no motive. We heard from Harry that he was innocent. Sally told us you got it all wrong."

"What are you saying?"

"Theo, I'm saying that you saw those two young people making love. Your precious

Barbara was having a terrific climax in Cliff Morton's arms. You were shocked as only a preadolescent child can be. You hated what you saw. You ran to the house and collected the gun. You knew how to use it. You went up into the hayloft and shot Cliff Morton yourself."

SIXTEEN

You won't be surprised to learn that I got up and walked out of the Annual Cure Hotel. Settled the bill, removed Alice Ashenfelter's rucksack from the car, dumped it in the hall, and drove off.

I think if any other driver on the A4 that evening had cut across me or just tried to hold the center, there'd have been blood on the road. I wasn't merely angry. It's a crimson blur in my memory.

I was through Chippenham before the rage turned inwards. I'd seen trouble coming and ignored it because it was blonde, nineteen, and willing to climb into my bed.

I'd taken the bait.

Too late now to race off down the A4. Escape was a delusion. She'd got it firmly into her mind that I'd killed her daddy, and she was out for blood. Never mind that I was nine at the time. I had to be made to suffer.

I had a fair idea how she'd arrange it. She'd run to Digby Watmore, her pet reporter. *News on Sunday* didn't need hard facts. They'd stitch me up with innuendo. Photos of the skull, a Colt .45, and me. And, somewhere down the page, Alice, sexy but soulful, captioned, "I found the murder weapon in Dr. Sinclair's house."

In the way of British justice seeking to right itself and keep its dignity, there would follow a protracted period of investigation, off the record for a while, then, in unhurried stages, handed over from police to lawyers to politicians. Grinding to the same tempo, the university would systematically strip me of my responsibilities, a tutor group here, a place on a committee there, loading me with extramural work at the expense of degree-level lecturing, until my position became untenable. Gently but inexorably easing me out.

Something had to be done about Alice.

I had to be positive.

I was home by nine. My first positive action was to pour myself a restoring Scotch and sink it fast. Then I went to the shelf in the hall where I kept the bills and junk mail and picked up something I'd placed there earlier: Digby Watmore's visiting card. I confirmed what I'd half remembered, that the fat reporter was a local man, a stringer. I took the card to the phone and called him.

Digby was at home. Yes, he remembered me. No, he wouldn't mind meeting me for a drink. Yes, he could get to Pangbourne in half an hour. He looked forward to seeing me in the lounge of the Copper Inn.

Considering that the last words I'd spoken to

him were "Sod off," he was either very forgiving or a true professional.

You'll find the Copper Inn in Egon Ronay, a trendy, well-appointed place, too classy for the likes of Digby, but I didn't want to be seen with him in my local. He was waiting for me just inside the door in his blue raincoat and green trilby. The small eyes shone with anticipation. There was a faint aroma of sweat. For a heavyweight he'd moved fast to get there before me.

No prizes for guessing that Digby was a beer drinker. I carried two pints to the table farthest from the bar.

Naturally, he wanted to know how Alice and I had spent the day.

I admitted we'd been to Somerset. Why deny it? One of my reasons for being here was to get my version in first.

Digby said nostalgically, "Recapturing those war years . . . Remember the Land Girls? I once went out with one. You wouldn't believe the muscles on her." Almost as an afterthought he asked, "Meet anyone you knew?"

"Bernard, the son. He didn't invite us in."

"So the Lockwoods are still there?"

"Apparently. We didn't meet the old farmer and his wife."

"Pity, they'd have made you welcome, I'm sure. How did the place look?"

"Smaller . . . and very muddy."

"You don't sound too enchanted, if you don't mind me mentioning it," commented Digby.

"It wasn't my idea of a day out," I said, adding quickly, "Alice thought of it."

Digby wobbled with amusement. "The eager Miss Ashenfelter. Extremely pretty girl, though. Worth doing a favor for, I daresay."

"I had no ulterior motive, if that's what you mean," I said tersely.

"Wouldn't dream of suggesting it, old boy," Digby assured me. "Not so much a favor as a reward, eh?"

I stared back and passed no comment.

"She *had* spent the night at your house when we called this morning, had she not?"

"True," I answered. "She arrived very late."

As a *News on Sunday* man, Digby's mind was on one track. "And after your day in the country together, is she taking a long, relaxing bath or warming up the bed?"

It seemed she hadn't phoned him yet. "I left her drinking coffee," I answered, declining to say where. "I'd like to ask you about Alice."

He grinned lewdly. "I wouldn't have thought there's much more to find out."

"On the contrary. She arrives from America and asks to see the *News on Sunday* files, and in no time at all she has a reporter and a photographer in tow. What's going on? Has she done a deal with you?"

"Not with me, old man. I take my instructions from London."

"Come on, what does the paper stand to get out of it?"

196

"A human-interest story. She's blonde, twenty years old, and the daughter of a convicted killer. She comes to England to find out about him. All good copy."

"There's more to it than that. You went to all the trouble of tracing me. Why? I was only a child in 1943."

"A key witness," said Digby.

"What do you want from me, then?"

"She asked to meet you."

"She's convinced that her father was wrongly convicted."

"Apparently."

"You don't seem at all surprised. I suppose the paper put her up to this."

Digby tried to look inscrutable.

I said with my anger held in check, "Doesn't your rag have any sense of responsibility? The girl is fanatical. She's loosing off some extraordinary accusations. At one stage today she even suggested I fired the fatal shot. A kid of nine."

"That is a bit over the top," Digby had the graciousness to say.

I hoped he would still feel the same when she put it to him herself. I added, "It's slanderous nonsense, and if I took it seriously, I'd want to know precisely how your paper is involved."

Digby dipped his mouth to the beer.

Having got that across, I said in a public-spirited vein, "What bothers me is that if there were grounds for doubting the Donovan verdict, this is not the right way to examine them."

197

"Possibly not," Digby conceded.

"As a crime reporter, you know the form," I went on. "Let's suppose some evidence turned up suggesting that a miscarriage of justice had occurred, and a man had been falsely convicted of murder. Hanged, in fact. Is there anything one could do within the law to clear his name?"

The fleshy mounds around Digby's eyes slid aside to reveal an interested gleam. "This is hypothetical?"

"Naturally."

"It would depend."

"On what?"

"In the first place, the quality of the evidence."

"Irrefutable."

Digby sniffed. "You'd be unwise to claim that it was. Are we speaking of forensic evidence, a new witness, or what?"

"Never mind. Let's say that the case for a new hearing was overwhelming."

He grinned. "It might overwhelm you or me, old sport, but try overwhelming the Home Office and see what happens."

"Is that the procedure? One applies to the Home Office?"

"You can try."

"You don't sound optimistic."

"I have personal knowledge of three families who've been sending in petitions for years."

"So what would you suggest?"

He drained his glass, peered at me artfully, and said, "I haven't enough to go on yet."

Waiting to be served, I took stock. Talking to the press goes against the grain, but I was damn sure Alice would be on to him in the morning.

Over that second pint I gave him a rapid rundown on the day's discoveries, stopping with our departure from the Royal Crescent. I didn't explain why Alice was spending the night in a seedy hotel in Bath. He listened and made no comment except a belch that I like to believe was inadvertent.

He must have felt he'd profited in some way, because he heaved himself off the chair to buy the next round. When he returned with the glasses, he asked what I proposed to do next.

"That's why I'm here," I explained. "Is there any point in pursuing this, opening old wounds, if it achieves nothing in the end?"

Digby pondered the question. "Candidly, the chances of getting a royal pardon for Donovan, if that's what you have in mind, are smaller than infinitesimal." He beamed. "Said that well after two pints, didn't I? It's a textbook case, as you know. Every lad who's passed through police college has heard of the skull in the cider."

"No one's questioning the work that was done on the skull," I pointed out.

"Ah, but it takes the gilt off the gingerbread if some bright chappy from Pangbourne proves that they got the wrong man in the end."

"True, but . . ."

"There's another thing. This is a jaundiced old pressman speaking, but let's not forget the international angle. Young American soldier helps us win the war and how do we show our gratitude. Wouldn't do much for the Atlantic alliance, would it? It's a hot potato, this one."

"You're saying we'd get nowhere through official channels?" Actually, it was what I'd expected him to say.

"Nothing short of a confession signed by the murderer would do any good." He emptied his glass again. "Mind you, that's only a personal opinion."

"So what do you suggest?"

Digby leaned back and displayed the triple-tiered flesh below his chin. "A direct appeal to Joe Public. It's the only sure way to win this one."

Playing dumb, I asked, "How would you go about it?"

"Through the paper — if we got that evidence."

I said in a low voice, "It's just possible I could obtain it. The real thing, not wild accusations."

His mouth jutted open, and a glassy look appeared in his eyes. The scoop of a lifetime was beckoning to Digby Watmore. "And you need some help from me?"

"No."

He reddened. "You and I could handle this together. No need to bring in the Fleet Street boys at this stage. We could come to terms, I'm certain. Generous terms."

"That's not important to me."

"What do you need, then?"

"Time. Two or three days without Miss Ashenfelter breathing down my neck."

"Then you'll give me an exclusive?"

I put out my right hand.

Digby smiled hugely and gripped it.

SEVENTEEN

Monday morning, ten A.M.

Twenty-six first-years looked expectantly towards me. On their syllabus sheets they had a lecture on the Venerable Bede scheduled for this hour. They were in for a disappointment.

Adhering to my belief that honesty is the best policy, I announced, "I'd better confess that I neglected to prepare this lecture. I spent the weekend with a blonde instead of Bede."

This was met with disbelieving jeers and a shout that I ought to be ashamed of myself.

"Indeed I am," I told them. "And to save my good name and reputation, I've brought in my slides of the great cathedrals and abbeys of Europe. Would you turn out the lights, Miss Hooper?"

Thank God for the great cathedrals and abbeys of Europe. My first reaction on waking at 8:50 A.M. had been to reach for the Alka-Seltzers and my slide projector. Just try ad-libbing for an hour on Bede.

When it was over, I made a phone call from the Senior Common Room. Sally Ashenfelter answered, reciting her number with a crispness that sounded encouragingly sober.

"This is Theo Sinclair," I told her. "Visited you yesterday, remember?" I was far from confident that she would.

"Why, yes. The evacuee. I'm afraid my husband isn't here this morning, Mr. Sinclair."

"Actually, I wanted to speak to you."

"Me?"

"We didn't have much time to talk. There were a couple of things I'm most anxious to ask you about."

"Oh?"

"I'm speaking from the university, Mrs. Ashenfelter. It's a little public here. Do you think we could meet?" I was about to say "For a drink," when empty vodka bottles clinked a warning in my head.

"In Bath, do you mean?" asked Sally.

"The Pump Room," I said on an impulse, "for a coffee."

She hesitated. "Which day did you have in mind?"

"How about tomorrow?"

"Let's see . . . Harry's going to be out all day, so that's all right. Someone's coming in the morning. I can't put them off." She thought a moment and suggested casually, "How about a lunchtime drink in the Francis?"

Alcoholics are smart operators. "Difficult," I said. "Afternoon tea in the Pump Room?"

She laughed. "Cucumber sandwiches, the three-piece orchestra and all? All right. Let's meet at three, before it gets too crowded."

"I'll have reserved a table," I promised.

I spent the next hour in the history department's library making up time.

Towards lunch, I scooped my books into a more tidy pile, walked down a staircase, through two sets of swing doors, and into the narrow office where a far-from-narrow secretary called Pippa received visitors to the psychology department. Pippa could pin you to the wall with one deep breath.

"Who's in today?" I asked. "The prof?"

Pippa shook her head, and it wasn't her head that moved most. "A conference at Liverpool."

"And Dr. Ott?"

"Just finished a seminar in room nineteen."

Simon Ott looked up in surprise when I found him rewinding a tape. I asked if he could spare a few minutes. We weren't well-known to each other, but that, for me, was an encouragement.

"I'm trying to clarify something slightly contentious," I explained.

"Concerning me?" A guarded expression dropped over his face like a visor. Small, neat, and in his thirties, he went in for dark suits and cream-colored shirts with one-color ties, that color generally being in the brown range.

"Me. I'm after advice."

"Ah." He looked marginally more approachable, then said, "I don't have much time. A meeting at two."

"Could I join you for lunch, perhaps?"

He glanced at my stick. "I generally take a walk."

"You think I wouldn't keep up?"

He hesitated. "If it doesn't concern me personally . . ."

"Your special field is the memory and how it functions, isn't it?"

The face did a double take. The mention of memory triggered an interested response, and the revelation that I'd made some inquiries about him turned him pink. Happily for me, curiosity prevailed. We compromised on a slow stroll across Whiteknights Park.

Without much preamble I told him what I remembered having seen in the small barn at Gifford Farm on Thanksgiving Day, 1943. I told him about Barbara's suicide, leaving out the murder and the trial. There was no need to go into all that sensational stuff. "The point is that I was required to make a statement," I said, letting him assume that it was for the inquest. "It's on record, so I can check my memory against what I said then. It hasn't altered. I can picture everything as I described it. What I saw was definitely a violent sexual attack. But quite recently someone has claimed that I gave an inaccurate account of what really took place — that in fact it was passionate lovemaking. There's some secondary evidence to back up this theory. I won't say it's shaken my confidence, because it hasn't."

"Why come to me, then?" Ott reasonably asked.

I flapped my hand vaguely. "There's that old saying about memory playing tricks."

He looked away, following the flight of some starlings to a mown stretch of grass near the Museum of Rural Life. "Tell me, did you know the people involved?"

"The girl, better than the man. He was virtually a stranger."

"But you knew her. Would you say that you liked her enough to identify emotionally with her?"

"Yes, I would."

"So this experience — whatever it was — must have distressed you?"

"Certainly. I was in tears."

We walked on for some way while he reflected on this. He resumed. "The brain has various defense mechanisms for coping with anxiety. We can, for example, repress certain stressful or disturbing memories by pushing them down into the unconscious."

I said, "That's a way of forgetting, isn't it? In my case we're talking about *remembering* something unpleasant."

"True."

"I mean, could I have been distorting the memory?"

"That's possible," said Ott. "The classic example was cited by Piaget, the Swiss psychologist, who remembered a man trying to kidnap him from his pram in the Champs-Elysées. His nurse managed to fight off the kidnapper and was scratched across the face. The man fled when a gendarme with a short cloak and white baton arrived. Piaget retained a sharp visual memory of the scene right into adolescence. When he was fifteen, his father received a letter from the nurse, who had long since left the family. She was joining the Salvation Army, and she wanted to confess something. In particular, she wanted to return the watch she'd been given as a reward for saving the child. The story was untrue. She'd given herself the scratches."

"So Piaget imagined it?"

"His explanation was that he must have heard the story from his parents and projected it into the past as a memory."

"What I saw definitely happened."

Ott didn't challenge my assertion. With the skill of the analyst he found a way of justifying it while raising serious doubts. "You must have heard accounts from other sources. It's not impossible that you modified your memory to fit someone else's version of what happened. Research suggests that memory isn't totally reliable. It's influenced by what we subsequently think. So a stressful memory might well be modified in retrospect. Do you often picture this scene of rape?"

We're getting into Freudian theory, I thought. He thinks I'm a sexual kink. "No. It's something I prefer not to think about."

"So you suppress it."

"Listen," I said, trying to sound reasonable.

"Aren't you missing the point? The scene I'm unable to visualize is this other nonviolent one, where they are actually lovers."

"Quite. And there's evidence to support it?"

"She was two months' pregnant. The facts point to the same guy who was with her in the barn."

He brooded silently. We'd turned and were approaching the Faculty of Arts building again. I was beginning to wish I hadn't bothered him.

Finally, he stopped and said, "There is a possible explanation. You were emotionally attached to the girl. You idolized her to some extent. It may be that the sight of her giving herself in love to a stranger was what really disturbed you. You couldn't accept it, so you invented a set of circumstances that left her blameless in your eyes. A rape was more acceptable than her complicity in the act of love." He studied me keenly with his pale eyes. "Is that a feasible interpretation?"

I pondered it. "You're saying I invented the rape to obliterate something that was even more unthinkable?"

"It's only a hypothesis."

"Is there any way I could test it?"

"You'd need the help of an analyst, I think. You see, it's possible that there are other factors at work."

"Such as?"

"Your feelings of guilt."

I felt a crawling sensation across my scalp. Had

he known all along about the Donovan case?

He explained, "You, presumably, raised the alarm when you found the couple together. The girl subsequently committed suicide. Perhaps you blame yourself."

I thanked him and said the discussion had been illuminating.

At one-thirty I went out to my car and drove out of Whiteknights Park and down Redlands Road to the main campus where the red-brick admin block and science labs were situated.

Having parked in the London Road, I unlocked the boot and took out a leather briefcase containing the Colt .45 that had been used to murder Cliff Morton. I carried it through the cloisters and into the physics lab. No one was inside. At the far end were two prep rooms. I was fortunate. The man I wanted, Danny Leftwich, was in there alone.

He put down his coffee. "Hey, what's this? Off limits, Dr. Sinclair?"

"Just slumming, Danny." There was a running battle about the antiquated facilities here, compared with our glass-and-concrete palace up at Whiteknights. Personally, I hankered after a return to the London Road site with its high ceilings and better ventilation, but it wasn't diplomatic to say so.

Danny offered me a coffee. We'd met often at the bridge table. He was the senior lab technician in the physics department, an intelligent man in his thirties, a polymath without the least

209

desire to earn a living lecturing students. He reckoned to polish off the crosswords in *The Times* and *The Telegraph* before lunchtime, in between supplying the technical needs of professors, lecturers, and research students. Each of the physics labs was superbly maintained, and Danny still found time to place bets for any of us who followed the horses.

On this occasion I was interested in another of Danny's enterprises: the university rifle and small-arms club. Through an enterprising and mysterious deal in 1961 with the horticulture department, he'd acquired a stretch of ground at Sonning and sufficient funds from the student union to build one of the best university ranges in the country. I wasn't a member of the club, but I'd been out there on a Sunday morning to see a match. The facilities and the way Danny managed them were a revelation.

I opened my case and took out Duke's pistol. "Seen anything like this before?" I asked him.

"The Colt automatic? If you don't mind, Dr. Sinclair . . ." He held out his left hand, and I placed the gun on his palm. "Always pick up a gun with the nonshooting hand." He removed the empty magazine and operated the slide to make a visual check of the breech. "No one's fired this in years. There's all kinds of gunge in here. Want me to clean it for you?"

"Please."

"Didn't know you were a gun man, Doc."

"You can see from the state of it, I'm not. It's

a relic, a souvenir. And please don't ask me if I have a certificate for it."

"What else have you got in there?" asked Danny as I delved into my case. "God, live ammunition!" He pointed to a sand bucket by the door. "On there, but gently. What is it — World War Two stuff?"

"No good now, I suppose?"

"I wouldn't care to fire it."

"Could you dispose of it for me?"

"Of course."

"Would the gun still be safe to use with some up-to-date ammunition?"

"Should be, after it's cleaned and oiled. I'll test-fire it if you like. Most of our pistol shooting is small-bore stuff, but I have a few boxes of .45s. Have you ever fired this thing?"

"Not for a long time. I was still in short trousers. Had to use both hands to control the recoil." I hesitated. "Could I be there when you test it?"

"If you can stand an early morning."

"How early?"

"Be at the range on Wednesday at eight A.M."

EIGHTEEN

The trio was playing a number from *Call Me Madam* as I entered the Pump Room. Appropriate, I thought: The carpeted area under the chandelier where teas were being served was entirely populated by sixtyish women in hats. A scattering of men, mostly blood-pressure cases in tweed suits, had taken up positions in armchairs by the windows, perusing copies of the morning papers clipped to wooden rods.

Ever since Beau Nash, the Pump Room formalities have been strictly observed. You waited for the lady with the pendant-pearl earrings to escort you to a Chippendale chair and hand you a menu. My request to be seated as far away from the music as possible was frigidly received, and when I said I wouldn't be ordering until my guest arrived, I was curtly informed that it was customary to wait for one's friends in the anteroom. I smiled and said yes, but I'd made other arrangements.

Two fifty-five by the grandfather clock. I was tense. The truth about Barbara might be hard to take. *"We had no secrets from each other,"* Sally had told me on Sunday, and I was prepared to

212

believe her. Back in those wartime days I'd watched her a number of times in earnest girl talk with Barbara, heads close, voices pitched low, eyes watchful for anyone who might over-hear.

I would ask Sally straight out whether Barbara and Duke had been lovers. Never mind that Harry had said "No chance" and practically throttled me for suggesting it. I wanted more convincing. I wouldn't believe I was mis-taken until I heard it from Sally.

Then the other question had to be put, cour-tesy of Alice and her theory. Sally might think it was in bad taste, but I would ask it because only she could tell me the answer. How had Barbara really felt about Cliff Morton? Everyone else had marked him down as a feckless, obnoxious character, and I was still at a loss to imagine her secretly preferring him to Duke.

Until I'd had it confirmed by Sally, I wasn't willing to believe that what I'd witnessed as a child in the hayloft was an act of love.

I'd spent a troubled night thinking over what Simon Ott had said about defense mechanisms. Without result. If only we could analyze the most highly charged moments of our childhood in a dispassionate way, psychiatrists wouldn't make such a good living. We hold rigidly to the impres-sions our minds retain, sometimes in the face of evidence to the contrary. I'd never seriously questioned what I believed I saw in 1943. It had become a fact, locked in and not to be disturbed.

I was still reluctant to give it an airing.

I didn't want to be told that I'd harbored a lie for over twenty years.

Well, if Sally confirmed that Barbara and Morton had been lovers, she had some explaining to do. Why hadn't she spoken up when the trial was held? True, she hadn't been called as a witness, but presumably she'd made statements to the police. Had she lied to them, or hadn't they asked her about Barbara's love life?

It crossed my mind that Sally's alcoholism could be due to a guilty conscience. It's hard to live with the knowledge that you might have saved an innocent man from the gallows.

Christ, I was getting morbid. Where was Sally?

Five minutes after three. I looked out towards the paved area of the Abbey churchyard. She was not in sight.

By 3:25, the place had filled up and I'd heard the trio's repertoire twice. The head waitress came over to ask how long I expected to occupy the table without ordering. I told her in a bored voice to bring a pot of tea for two and some cakes.

At 3:50, a queue had formed just inside the door. I watched an exchange between the head waitress and the girl who'd brought my order. The bill was brought to my table without my asking for it. I topped up my teacup, waited for another rendering of *Call Me Madam*, settled my bill, and joined the newspaper readers by the window.

I decided to give her until 4:10, even though I didn't expect to see her now. Too late, I reflected that I should have agreed to meet at the Francis for that lunchtime drink. Then she'd at least have had an incentive.

So I left the Pump Room, collected my car, and drove up to the Royal Crescent where I saw for myself why Sally had failed to keep the appointment.

Her house was gutted.

A fire engine and a police car were drawn up on the cobbles opposite. A few people were standing around outside but there was no activity. It had all happened earlier in the afternoon. The stonework above the first-floor windows was charred to the level of the balustrade. Every pane was smashed, each frame burned out. The debris lay in a pool of black water in the basement. The lower walls and parts of the adjoining frontage were saturated to a deep mustard color.

I came to a screeching stop beside the fire engine, explained to the men in the cab that I was a friend of the people who lived there, and asked when the fire had happened.

"We took the call at 2:13," one told me.

"Was anyone . . . ?"

"One woman taken to the Royal United. Unconscious. Pretty bad, I'm afraid."

"Where is it?"

He told me, and I raced the MG through the afternoon traffic at actionable speed.

I parked in the doctor's bay. Casualty Reception sent me upstairs. The first person I saw was Harry.

He was slumped on a steel-and-canvas chair outside the Intensive Care Unit, pressing his knuckles against his teeth. He looked up at me and said in a hollow voice. "What the heck?"

"I went to the house and they told me. What's happening?"

"She's unconscious. Asphyxia. Third-degree burns. I don't want to see her like that."

"Do they hold out any hope?"

"No one's saying. I haven't been here long. Out all day. Got back around four and saw what happened. God!"

"Any idea of the cause?"

Harry turned to look at me. "You trying to be funny, mister? She's a dipso. She smokes. Okay?"

"Have they said she was drinking?"

"They said nothing."

Out of consideration I did the same. I disliked the man, but this wasn't the time to question his logic. I sat opposite him and tried to catch up with my thoughts. I know there are all kinds of theories about coincidences, but it was incredible to me that this should happen on the afternoon Sally had promised to meet me. I wanted to know the cause of that fire.

We waited some twenty minutes before a doctor came out. He'd slipped his face mask down. Harry had his head bowed, so the doctor caught my eye and said in a voice too stiltedly considerate to be bringing good news, "Mr. Ashenfelter?"

I inclined my head towards Harry.

NINETEEN

The bad news wasn't over. On the stairs, my way was barred by a busybody in a brown suit. He raised his hands, palms facing me, in an officious manner that I thought was a shade excessive for the National Health Service. Probably a nut case, I decided.

He said, "Hey."

To humor him I nodded as I stepped sideways.

He put his hands on my arm and said, "We'd like a few words with you."

"Who are *we?*" I asked.

He produced from his pocket a card in a plastic folder. "Detective-Inspector Voss, CID, Bath Police."

I gave it a glance. It appeared to be an authentic police identity. I raised my face. Looked right into his brown eyes under thick black smudges of eyebrow. I'd read somewhere that policemen attach a lot of importance to the way our eyes first react to theirs. If you blink and look at the back of your hand, they start filling in the charge sheet.

When I reckoned I'd passed that test, I took in the rest: the squat nose, the lumpy chin, and the muscled neck that looked ready for a scrum-down. Quite ten years older than I, yet in good shape physically. A fit forty. Not one to raise my stick to.

He said, "Is that your MG outside?" and for an optimistic moment I wondered if this was simply a complaint about the place I'd chosen to park in.

It wasn't. He wanted me to drive behind his car to the central police station.

I asked, "What's this about, exactly?"

"You'll find out."

"Do you want to know what I'm doing here?" I asked, prepared to be cooperative. "I can tell you that now. We don't need to go to the police station."

He eyed me as he decided between asserting brute authority and providing a reason. Either way, he wasn't amenable to suggestions from me. "This is the casualty department of a hospital. They don't want us here, getting in their way."

So we drove in convoy to the station where I parked beside his Triumph and followed him in-side. Give the police their due, they found me a cup of coffee in a paper cup before they left me on a bench in front of a notice board. I may be cynical, but I interpreted that to mean that I was in for a long wait, and I was right. I spent an hour and twenty minutes with the notice board. By the time I was called, I could have passed an exam on foot-and-mouth disease or the Colorado beetle.

Inspector Voss had removed his jacket and looked ready to take on the All Blacks football team at Twickenham single-handedly. From the angle I had in the chair in front of his desk, he was hunched forward with his shoulders at the level of his ears. It was some comfort to have a uniformed man seated in the corner behind me, though I could have taken that as a bad sign.

I was right about the aggressive posture. He started with a head-down charge. No apology for keeping me waiting. Just: "I've been hearing things about you, Dr. Sinclair."

"From Harry Ashenfelter, I suppose."

He tensed and pulled back a fraction.

I explained, "He must have given you my name."

He said with derision, "This is the CID, chum. We're not incapable of finding out a man's name."

"By asking Harry Ashenfelter?"

He thrust his jaw forward aggressively. "How long have you known Mr. Ashenfelter?"

"I met him twenty-one years ago when he was with the American Army, based at Shepton Mallet."

"And since?"

I hesitated. If only to keep this inquisition to a minimum, I didn't want the entire story to come out now, yet I couldn't be sure how much Harry had said already. "Last Sunday afternoon I visited him and his wife. The first time since the war. His stepdaughter, Alice, had called on me, and I helped her to find Harry in Bath."

"A family reunion, then?"

"In a way."

"So Alice is a friend of yours?"

I sidestepped that one. "She just turned up at the university where I work — that's Reading — and made herself known to me."

"Why didn't she go straight to Bath?"

"Didn't have their address."

Voss curled his lip in disbelief. "Didn't have her stepfather's address?"

"I gather he walked out on her mother years ago and they lost touch."

"So she met Mrs. Ashenfelter — the lady who died in the fire — for the first time on Sunday?"

"Correct."

While we were talking, he'd picked up a pencil and inscribed a thick, asymmetrical circle on the notepad in front of him. Now he lifted the pencil off the sheet and jabbed it down heavily in the center. "Let's talk about you. You'd met Sally Ashenfelter before." He expressed it as a statement.

"When I was a child."

"Of what age?"

"Nine."

"The circumstances?"

"It was the war. I was evacuated to her village. She happened to work on the farm where I stayed."

"Where does Harry Ashenfelter fit in?"

"He was a visitor to the farm, helping with the harvest. A GI."

Voss inched his face closer to mine to add impact to his next observation. "The friend of the GI who murdered Clifford Morton."

If it was calculated to throw me, it didn't succeed. He was a policeman, after all. He would have been pretty incompetent if he hadn't made the connection. I simply gave a nod and returned his look.

He said as if he were accusing me of something, "You were the boy who gave evidence for the prosecution."

"An unsworn statement."

"And twenty years later you come back to Somerset with Alice Ashenfelter in tow, disturbing people with all kinds of questions about the case."

I said, "Why should anyone be disturbed?"

By the way of a response he treated me to a gratuitous bit of nostalgia. "Matt Judd handled that case. I learned my trade with him. He was God to me."

Remembering Superintendent Judd, I commented, "He put the fear of God into me."

Voss brought his hands together in a reverential gesture with the fingers interlocking. "The finest nicker the West Country ever produced."

"Always managed to pin it on someone?"

The wistful expression twitched into a scowl. "Remember where you are, sunny Jim."

I checked my watch ostentatiously. "I'm not likely to forget."

With a grave stare he warned me, "You don't

appear to understand how serious this is. I'd better acquaint you with the facts. That fire up at the Crescent. On the face of it you'd think it was a straight case of a tipsy woman chucking a cigarette into a waste bin and sending the place up in flames. Not so simple. The lads from the fire service found Sally Ashenfelter lying in the living room where the fire started. Evidence of heavy smoking and heavy drinking, yes. Fire appears to have started in a waste bin, yes. But things were stacked around that bin, Dr. Sinclair. Flammable things. Bits of wooden furniture, magazines, some African ornaments carved in ebony, a cigar box —"

"It was arson, you mean?" I cut in.

"Murder," said Voss, watching me interestedly, waiting to see me squirm after he'd put the boot in. He'd learned his trade from Superintendent Judd.

I said automatically as my mind raced through the implications, "This is certain?"

"It has to be confirmed, but I'm satisfied with what I saw up there."

"You don't think she might have moved those things herself?"

"Suicide?" He shook his head. "She was awash with vodka. Paralytic." He glanced towards the policeman in the corner. "Did you ever hear of anyone killing themselves like that?"

I didn't turn my head to check the response.

Voss picked up the pencil again and prodded the air with it to punctuate his next speech.

"How about the other thing? Someone visits the lady, knowing she's an alcoholic, gets her drinking vodka until she's out to the world, then makes a bonfire of the furniture, drops a cigarette into the bin, and leaves. How's that for a hypothesis?"

I said, "Don't ask me. You're the detective."

The pencil snapped in his hand.

For a moment I thought he was going to reach across the desk and grab me, but he took a deep breath and said with a show of self-control that strained him to the limit, "All right, my friend, I'll ask you this instead. What were you doing in Bath today?"

"Waiting in the Pump Room most of the time. I'd arranged to meet Sally Ashenfelter at three."

"Again? You said you saw her on Sunday."

"Not for long. She was, em . . . indisposed before the end of the visit."

"Smashed out of her mind?"

"A fair description," I admitted.

"So you knew about Sally's drinking?" The image of the rugby forward was right for Voss; he was all intimidation and thrust.

"So did half of Somerset, I imagine," I said, gathering it and booting it back. "Alcoholics aren't known for their discretion." Encouraged, I said, "I wouldn't have waited in the Pump Room for practically an hour and a half if I'd known she was at the bottle this morning."

Voss didn't seem particularly impressed. "What time did you arrive in Bath?"

"About two-thirty."

"Where were you at one-thirty?"

"On the road from Reading."

"Did you stop anywhere? Petrol? A spot of lunch?"

"No. I drove straight here."

"And before that?"

"I was at home, preparing a lecture."

Voss eased back in his chair and took a long, speculative look at me. "We'll have to take your word for that, won't we? The fire was started between one and two, when you say you were on the road." The disbelief he managed to put into that word, *say*, was an obvious taunt.

I refused to rise to it.

When it had sunk in that I was unwilling to respond, he said, "You'd better tell me what was behind this meeting with Mrs. Ashenfelter."

Tricky. He wouldn't be overjoyed to hear doubts raised about his idol Judd's most triumphant case. I stalled a little. "There was nothing sinister in it, I can assure you, Inspector. Just that she said enough before she started on the vodkas on Sunday to make me think it would be profitable to speak to her again. I had the feeling she'd have more to say if her husband wasn't listening, so I phoned her up and arranged to meet."

His eyes narrowed. "More to say about what?"

I answered offhandedly, "Nothing in particular."

"I want a better answer than that," said Voss, gritting his teeth.

225

"Really," I insisted, "it wouldn't have mattered what she talked about." I'd decided that diversionary tactics were necessary here, and to be convincing I needed to let Inspector Voss flounder a little first.

He warned me, "You'd better not play silly buggers with me."

I said with high seriousness, "I'm trying to explain that what Mrs. Ashenfelter said was of less importance to me than *how* she said it." The mystification written across his features was gratifying, but I sensed that it might have been dangerous to prolong it, so I added, "She's a Somerset woman, lived in the county all her life, and uses dialect words that I first heard twenty years ago, long before I trained as a medieval historian. I don't specialize in philology" — kidology, more like, I thought in passing — "but there are obvious points of contact." Watching the indecision in his eyes, I decided that the tutorial method was more appropriate here than a lecture. "Now you, as a Somerset man, must have heard of the word *dimpsy*, for example, for twilight."

Voss gave a guarded nod.

I said, "Did you know it's straight from the Anglo-Saxon *dimse?* Fascinating, isn't it, to find the word surviving in the dialect? Just one example of the sort of thing I had ambitions of exploring with Sally Ashenfelter's help."

Voss said in a voice that was not yet convinced but more than halfway there, "You're telling me you arranged to meet her to talk about words?"

"Precisely," I said encouragingly. "I can give you other examples if you like." My mind ran rapidly through the few I'd retained. It was a long time since I'd compiled those lists for Duke.

"Don't bother," he told me.

"Someone has to," I persisted, playing the zealous academic with all the conviction at my command. "Many of these old expressions will be irretrievably lost if no one cares about them, Inspector." I launched into an impassioned appeal for the collection and preservation of sound archives.

He cut me off in mid-sentence. "I haven't time to listen to you rabbiting on about words. I'm investigating a suspected murder." But for all his bluster he'd lost his grip on the interview. He wasn't in Judd's class. His next question was more of an appeal than a demand. "Is there anything else you can tell me that might assist me in my inquiries?"

I let him wait. If I played this right, I could be out of here in a few minutes. I screwed up my face and rubbed my chin thoughtfully. Finally, I said, "It may be unimportant, but when I phoned Sally to arrange a meeting, she said she couldn't see me in the morning because someone was coming."

He seized on it. "She was expecting someone? Who?"

"She didn't say."

"A man?"

"I've no idea. All she told me was that someone was coming in the morning and she couldn't put them off."

He got up from his chair to pace the room, beating his fist repeatedly into the palm of his left hand. "A visitor. The husband didn't mention a visitor."

"Maybe he wasn't told."

This prompted Voss to clap his hand to the back of his neck. "A secret visitor. Someone she didn't mention to her husband. Who? A lover?" He sounded encouraged, then pressed his hand to his forehead. "But why should the lover want to kill her?"

I listened in a bored way and took a look at my watch.

"This opens it up," said Voss. "By Jesus, it opens it up!"

I cleared my throat. "Have you finished with me?"

Voss looked at me abstractedly. "Finished? For the present, yes. Have we got your address?"

"I gave it to the sergeant at the desk."

"Fair enough." He made a dismissive gesture.

I didn't say good-bye as I went out.

TWENTY

Pressure.

I'd tried ignoring it, turning my back on it, meeting it halfway, laughing in its face, arguing with it, defying it, but still it closed in, unstoppable. Now it had got to me.

I needed the gun.

From Bath I drove fast along the Wiltshire roads, main beam probing the evening mist, wipers working intermittently. I kept checking the mirror, because I had a suspicion that I was being tailed. One set of headlamps stayed consistently fifty yards behind me whatever speed I was doing, and at times I was going flat out.

The victim of my own imagination?

No. The threat of pursuit was real. I was suspected of murder. Doubly suspected. First Alice had pointed the finger at me. Now Inspector Voss.

You may think I was overreacting to Alice's charge of shooting Cliff Morton in 1943, that it was too absurd to take seriously. But I'd learned enough about that young woman in the last five days to regard her as dangerous. She kept nothing to herself. It was a sure bet that she'd mouthed her suspicions to Digby Watmore by now. With the press on to me, as well as the police, what chance would I have?

Two murders down to me. Put them together and *News on Sunday* would have a field day. I'd be in the same league as Heath and Christie.

Each time I drove through a stretch lit by street lamps I slowed and tried to identify the car trailing me. Difficult, because he kept his distance, and the mist lingered right into Berkshire, but by degrees I reached a few conclusions. A large black limousine with a wide axis and low lines, possibly a Jaguar, driven by a man, no passengers.

At Thatcham I stopped for petrol. While the girl was unfastening the cap I stepped quickly into the road to see what my faithful follower would do. Nowhere in sight. Yet two minutes after I got on the road again, I checked the mirror, and he was back with me.

On familiar territory, where the A340 forks left to Pangbourne, I slipped the leash by turning sharp left a short way up the road towards Englefield Park, then left again by the lake and back to the A4. I believe he overshot at the first turn.

I switched my thoughts to more useful activity. I'd arranged with Danny Leftwich to pick up the Colt .45 at the range on Wednesday morning, only I couldn't wait that long. He should have finished cleaning it by now. So I drove past Reading on the A4 almost as far as

Sonning and then branched right to seek out Danny's sixteenth-century cottage by the golf course. I'd played bridge there several times the previous winter.

My lights first picked out the hump of his Volkswagen above a low stone wall, then the squat structure of the thatched cottage. Smoke, coiling into the night sky from one of the two chimneys, encouraged me; the unlit interior didn't. I stopped by the wall, followed the winding route between soggy lavender bushes to the front door, touched the bellpush, heard it chime two notes, and waited hopefully. A dog barked. Nothing else.

No point in trying the bell again. Between the chimes and the barking, most of Sonning must have heard that Danny Leftwich had a visitor. I should have guessed that a man of Danny's energy didn't spend his nights indoors in front of the TV. Looking around, I spotted a brick-built garage or workshop at the end of the garden.

One thing was clear: He didn't expend much of that energy in the garden. It was a job finding the crazy paving in the long grass. Worth it, though. When I rapped the door, Danny's voice piped up at once, "Who is it?"

I told him.

He called, "Hold on, Theo. I'll be right with you."

I waited over a minute, then the door opened and I got a whiff of the chemicals and understood why the delay had been necessary. The building was a photographic darkroom. I had to bend my head to avoid touching a set of still wet prints pegged to plastic lines.

"Not bad, hm?" he said as I glanced at them.

They were nude shots. One shot, to be accurate, a blowup in black and white, printed ten times over. So-called glamour photography. A girl bending slightly forward, head turned to look over her shoulder at the camera, as if in a relay race, except that her bottom was too plump for a runner, and her pouting expression suggested it wasn't a baton she was looking out for.

"Something new in cottage industries," I commented.

"My spinning wheel's got woodworm," said Danny.

"I suppose you've got an outlet for these?"

There was a glint of mischief from Danny as he said, "Rikky Patel."

I winced in disbelief. Rikky was another of our bridge team, an unfailingly solemn senior technician in the biology department.

"Rikky goes in for this?"

He enjoyed the idea for a moment and then explained, "Rikky's uncle is a publisher. The Indian subcontinent is a fabulous market for soft porn." He poured the contents of a developing tray into a beaker. "Come for your gun? I thought we said Wednesday."

"Is it ready? You're a pal."

Danny wiped his hands and led me out and

through the lavender to the cottage. The Colt was lying on a cloth on the kitchen table among a collection of bristle brushes, screwdrivers, jags, allen keys, cocktail sticks, and tins of gun oil. He picked it up and operated the slide. "I haven't adjusted the sights. I was hoping to test-fire it."

"I know," I told him. "Something has come up. Did you by any chance get hold of some . . ."

"New cartridges? Sure. They'll cost you a bit."

I paid him generously, and nothing was said about the use I expected to make of them. "As a matter of interest," I asked him, "the Colt is a pretty heavy weapon, isn't it? I mean, the recoil is something to reckon with."

"It has that reputation," he agreed.

"Do you reckon a boy of nine could handle it with any accuracy?"

He frowned.

"I know it's against the law," I said, "but just supposing it happened."

He gave me a puzzled look and said, "Theo, you already told me you fired the thing two-handed when you were a boy."

Stupid, I thought. Of course I mentioned it last time. Too much on my mind.

I told him, "That was just messing about in a field, shooting at a tin can."

He gave a shrug and we left it at that.

Although it was spotting with rain, he insisted on coming out to the car with me. Before I switched on, he made it obvious that there was something he wanted to mention. He bent his head confidentially to the window.

To be frank, I was slightly annoyed. I thought I'd made it plain that I wouldn't land him in trouble with the law. He'd done me a favor, I'd paid him handsomely, and the matter was closed. So before he got a word out, I said forcefully, "Great to have friends you can trust, Danny. Thanks, mate." I started up.

But he insisted on saying something else. He had to shout above the MG's engine note. "She's a bit sensitive about the posing. You won't let on that you know about it, will you?"

I said without understanding, "Of course not."

I was back on the A4 more than a mile from the cottage when it dawned on me. That's how preoccupied I was with my own predicament. I had to make a profound mental effort to visualize the naked girl in the photograph. When I did, I whistled, not so much at the shock of identity as at Danny's enterprising genius. She *was* familiar, but in another setting, seated at her typewriter in a white blouse and pleated skirt, the elegant secretary of the history department, Carol Dangerfield.

Bully for you, Carol, I thought. *Don't worry, I can keep a secret.*

With the gun in my pocket and an empty road behind me, I felt better than I had all day. It lasted only as long as it took me to drive home.

The black Jaguar that had followed me from Bath was parked in my driveway. I thought about slamming the car into reverse and leaving him to it. I thought about the newspapers. I thought about the police. In the end I drew up beside the Jaguar, switched off, took out the gun and the box of cartridges Danny had given me, slotted six of them into the magazine, and pressed it home. Then I heard the crunch of shoes on gravel. I thrust the Colt into my jacket pocket a split second before the car door was grabbed and swung open.

"Out, jerk."

I knew the voice. Didn't need to look any higher than the stubby hand gripping the two-foot length of lead piping from my garage.

"What's this about?" I asked Harry Ashenfelter as my heart pumped in double time.

"Give me that."

I handed my walking stick to him, and he slung it far into the darkness of the garden.

"Now get out."

I said, "You're crazy."

He swung the piping high and cracked it down on the bonnet of the car. Chips of red paint hit the windscreen.

I said, "You'll pay for that."

He lifted it again.

This time I did as he'd ordered, using my arms and good leg to achieve the vertical. Propped against the car, I faced him. "Now what?"

He jerked his head in the direction of the house.

I said, "Difficult."

"Brother, I don't care if you have to crawl on your belly."

It didn't come to that. By lolloping along the side of the car, I shunted myself from the MG to the Jaguar and then, with a couple of hops, to the storm porch. Felt for my key and let myself in.

Harry was close behind me, making sure I didn't slam the door on him. I switched on the hall light and kept my momentum going as far as the living room. Sank into an armchair and in the same movement slipped the Colt automatic from my coat pocket and wedged it handily between my right thigh and the side of the chair, twisting my body so that he was unsighted.

He switched on the main light and pulled the cord on the curtains. He was crimson with emotion or anger or sadistic anticipation. He crossed the room and stood over me, holding the pipe horizontally against my neck and forcing my jaw upwards. "Now, punk," he said, giving me a faceful of his sour breath, "you better tell me why you set fire to my home and murdered my wife."

His priorities were instructive, but I thought it prudent not to comment. I couldn't speak, anyway, with the piping jammed against my larynx. I made a strangled sound, and he eased the pressure enough for me to say, "I had nothing to do with the fire, for God's sake. I gave the police a full account of my movements."

"Crap," said Harry.

"True! I was on the road when the fire started."

"How'd you know when it started?"

"From the police. Listen, Harry, I had no

reason to harm Sally. I had an appointment to meet her this afternoon. I was waiting in the Pump Room over an hour."

"Making sure you were seen, huh?"

"Balls."

He rocked my head back with the bar and jammed a knee into my stomach. With the reflex I practically decapitated myself. I vomited. He drew back and cuffed me with the back of his right hand. I doubled up, groaning.

He said close to my ear, "So help me, creep, I'm going to have the truth out of you."

I asked for water.

He hit me across the face again. My lip split, and warm blood oozed down my chin.

He shouted, "Sit up!"

I did as he commanded, pressing my shoulders against the back of the chair.

Harry had boobed. He'd stepped back to admire his work. And now he saw a Colt. 45 leveled at his chest. His hands tightened on the lead piping.

"Drop it," I said. "This is in good nick, and loaded."

His face twitched and turned gray, but he obeyed.

I said, "Back against the wall, facing me."

I had a clear line of fire from the chair.

I said as evenly as circumstances allowed, "Maybe now I can get some sense out of you. Apparently, you believe I started the fire. Why?"

Silence. He was drained of aggression.

"Lost your voice? Touch of laryngitis?"

He wetted his lips nervously. Panic had manifestly set in.

By contrast, I was back to my sarcastic best. "Don't tell me you're one of those jumpy types who can't look into the barrel of a gun and talk rationally."

"Don't shoot," he finally managed to say, adding limply, "You'll regret it."

"Come off it, Harry. I've got a right to defend myself from a thug like you."

"With a murder weapon?" he said frenziedly. "I know that gun. It's a U.S. Army automatic, the one the police never found after Morton was shot. Tell me it isn't."

Honest, as usual, I shrugged and said nothing.

Harry was back in business as a communicator. He started talking fast on a high, hysterical note. "I know about you, Sinclair. You're in real trouble now. You must be out of your mind. I guess you flipped when Alice turned up out of nowhere wanting to dig up the past. It was all buried and forgotten, tidy and grassed over. You live in style now, this smart place in the country, a good job in the university. No one here knows about your past."

"What past?"

"Like blowing Morton's brains out with that thing in your hand."

I stared back at him with supreme indifference. I'd listened to the buildup, in no doubt about what was coming. Harry Ashenfelter was

238

just one more self-appointed amateur detective out to shock.

"You killed the guy," he said superfluously, his big scene in ruins around him, "and you let my buddy swing for it." Sensing the need to tone it down, he put up a quivering hand. "Okay, you were just a kid at the time. Under pressure. All that. I give you all that. You could get help, you know. You need a good lawyer."

I sighed. He was pathetic.

He said with all the concern he could register in that lumpy, combative face, "Did you know Sally was actually sorry for you? She told me you got Barbara Lockwood all wrong."

I reminded him wearily, "I heard this from you on Sunday. It doesn't mean I shot Cliff Morton."

Harry showed no sign of having heard. He was too keyed-up to draw any kind of deduction. The words were gushing from him on the Scheherazade principle, in a breathless bid to stop me from pulling the trigger. "Sally and I did some serious talking since. She told me things I didn't know. Nobody knew but Sally. Jesus Christ, is it any wonder she was an alcoholic?"

"What things did she tell you?"

"About Barbara. Barbara's secrets."

My mouth suddenly felt drained. Trying to sound unconcerned, I said, "Oh, yes?"

"Listen to this, Sinclair. Barbara was nuts on Morton. She really loved the guy. She was carrying his baby."

Pulses started throbbing in my head. It isn't easy after twenty years to accept that you were totally wrong about someone you would have gone to the wall for. I'd heard this from Alice, but she couldn't have known for certain. She'd guessed about Barbara and Morton, and I hadn't believed her. Deep down I'd felt sure that Sally would expose it as a cruel defamation.

But it wasn't. Barbara, my Barbara, had misled me. She'd used me to promote the lie that she wanted Duke. I was forced to accept it now.

I said in a dry, distant voice, "Barbara told Sally this?"

"Sure." Harry locked one of his forefingers over the other and said, "Those two girls were like this. Barbara confided to Sal that she let Cliff Morton make it with her whenever he wanted. But old man Lockwood and his lady didn't care for Morton at all. He was bad news."

"That part is true," I admitted. "What else?"

"They ordered Barbara to stop seeing the guy. This was after George Lockwood caught them together."

"In the orchard?"

"Right. Barbara was shattered. The poor kid was pregnant, and on top of that, Morton's call-up papers had just arrived. Then Morton came up with a plan. He wasn't a total jerk. He offered to marry the girl. He figured he could dodge the call-up by taking Barbara to Ireland. Neutral territory. She could marry him there and have the baby." Harry paused for breath, studying my reception of the story. I must have looked pole-axed. "This is on the level, Sinclair."

"Is that all?"

He wound himself up again. "Hell, no. There's more. They had to get new identities. Morton knew a guy in the Town Hall who said he would fix it in a matter of days if the money was right. Then they'd find a boatman along the Bristol Channel willing to ship them to Ireland. Meantime, Morton needed a place to lay up. So Barbara came up with a suggestion. She said he could hide in one of the barns on the farm. She'd keep him supplied with food. And that's what happened."

I screwed up my face in disbelief. "He was there on the farm?"

"Right up to the day you shot him."

I was so stunned by the information that I allowed the remark to stand. Harry had got the dumb, undivided attention he wanted.

"Barbara was smart. She encouraged her parents to think she was seeing Duke, and they didn't mind too much. In their eyes anyone was better than Morton, even a GI." A nervous grin streaked across his lips. "People generally locked up their daughters when the Yanks hit town. Not the Lockwoods. Barbara put it around that she had something going with Duke. As you know, she went out with him a couple of times. And she used you to stoke up the story."

And I'd repeated it at Duke's trial. My skin prickled. "Did Sally tell you that or are you embroidering?"

"She had it from Barbara. Gospel truth. You got to believe it."

I did. I knew, sickeningly, resoundingly, that it was true. I'd been pitchforked into a living hell. My discredited evidence had helped to hang an innocent man.

At last Harry had dried up. The next move was up to me, and I was in no shape for action. He sensed the softening in my resolve, or just the wish to be rid of him and work things out for myself, because his eyes traveled upwards from the gun. He was assessing his chances of getting out alive.

Stalemate.

I wouldn't shoot him in cold blood, but it wasn't safe to lower the gun. He couldn't move and neither could I, without my stick. I couldn't even escort him to his car and send him on his way.

Rashly, through my tormented emotions, I grasped at reason. Harry believed I'd shot Morton and killed Sally.

I said, "Do me the favor of answering one straightforward question. If Morton was Barbara's lover, why would I have shot him?"

"Jealousy."

"For Christ's sake. I was in short trousers."

"I was there. Remember?" said Harry, picking up confidence by the second. "You had a crush on the girl, right? Puppy love. I saw it. Sally saw it. Barbara used it. Her fatal mistake. Never mess with a kid's emotions."

I said heatedly, bitterly, "What am I supposed to have done? Shot Morton in a jealous passion and cut up the body? At nine years old? Who are you kidding?"

Harry was sounding more in control than I. "No," he said evenly. "Duke disposed of the body. He took pity on you."

"What?"

"He was like a father to you. He'd do anything to get you off the hook. He drove back to the farm that night, hacked off the head and put it in the cider barrel, and then transported the rest someplace else, miles away."

I was practically speechless. "He didn't tell you that."

"No. But it has to be true. It was typical of the guy. He adored kids."

"It doesn't *have* to be true at all."

Harry was determined to complete the explanation. "When they finally caught up with him, he refused to put the finger on you. Stupid and brave. That was Duke Donovan."

"And you think I kept silent at the trial?" I shouted at him as my anger erupted. "Allowed them to hang the man who's supposed to have saved me? What kind of vicious bastard do you take me for? If I could have thought of *anything* to stop them hanging Duke, I'd have spoken up."

"The guy was innocent," said Harry. "I told you he was innocent."

"I *know*. It breaks my heart. It's monstrous. Hideous. But I didn't know at the time. For twenty years I swallowed the story that he was guilty. I'm bloody certain now that he wasn't, and I'm going to find the killer. I don't know for sure who it was, but I know where to go."

A pause.

"The farm?"

I nodded and made a superhuman effort to sound rational. "Do you know why I'm so certain?"

"Sally?"

"Yes. She was killed because of what she would have told me."

"You think whoever murdered Morton also . . ."

"Right."

We faced each other in a tense, thoughtful silence, each wiser yet with our impasse unresolved. I could have said more. I elected not to. What I'd expressed was spontaneous, impassioned, and enough.

Finally, Harry took the initiative. He said, "Okay, my friend, call me crazy, but I believe you. If I'm right that you didn't kill Morton or Sally, I don't have to worry. You won't shoot me. So I'll tell you what I'm going to do. I'm going to walk right out of here, get in my car, and drive away. Understand?"

I gave a nod.

He wanted extra assurance. "You're not planning to stop me? In that case, would you lower the gun?"

This, in essence, was what the superpowers had debated ever since Hiroshima. There had to be some trust between us. Disarmament was the only sane way forward. I glanced down and put my good foot on the lead piping he'd threatened me with. I stared at Harry. Then I slowly planted the gun on my lap and placed my hands on the arms of the chair.

Harry dipped his head in recognition, took a couple of tentative sideways steps, and started across the room towards the door. I followed him with my eyes, making no move.

A sitting duck.

It happened at speed, though I see it now in slow motion. He was practically behind me and through the door when his right hand grabbed something off the top of the filing cabinet there.

A multicolored glass paperweight about the size of a cricket ball but twice as heavy.

An arc of light at the edge of my vision. The thing in his hand streaking towards my head.

The crunch.

Nothing.

TWENTY-ONE

A ringing sound.

Shrill, insistent, and painful.

I opened my eyes and saw daylight seeping into the space above the curtains. Fingered the swelling at the back of my skull. Groaned.

The ringing wasn't all in my head.

At some stage of the night I'd emerged from unconsciousness sufficiently to drag myself as far as the sofa and collapse there. Now I was cold, my clothes were clammy, and I needed about a dozen aspirins.

I groped for my stick. It wasn't there, of course. I made the effort to roll off the sofa and crawl to the phone.

Picked it up and listened.

"Ah, so all life is not extinct in Pangbourne. Is this the ear of Dr. Theodore Sinclair?" A man's voice, resonant, bombastic, pleased with itself. The voice that could spell *diarrhea* without the aid of a dictionary.

"Who else?"

"This is Watmore, Digby Watmore. I suppose I got you out of bed."

"No. What time is it?"

"Eight-twenty or thereabouts. Wednesday. Two or three days without, you said."

"Two or three days without what?"

"Miss Ashenfelter on your back, to quote you verbatim. Don't tell me you've forgotten. We made an agreement."

I recalled it faintly, as if from another incarnation. "When was this, Digby?"

"Sunday evening. The last two days have been no picnic for me, I can assure you. I say, are you sure I haven't disturbed your sleep?"

"What happened to Miss Ashenfelter?"

He gave what sounded like an exasperated snort. "She's been my constant companion for the past forty-eight hours."

"Day and night, Digby?"

"I put my studio couch at her disposal, but she prefers to pass the night having interminable conversations about the Donovan case."

I yawned sympathetically. "Was it instructive?"

"That's beside the point now," said Digby testily. "Events have overtaken us, haven't they?"

"Quite a lot has happened, yes."

"That's precisely why I'm on the line. A fine shock I had this morning, picking up the *Western Morning Press* and reading about this fire in Bath. Have you seen it?"

"The paper? No."

"Did you know about the fire? The Ashenfelters' place gutted. Mrs. Ashenfelter dead."

"Er . . . yes. I was in Bath."

There was a moment's offended silence.

"Well, thanks for sweet F.A., Sinclair."

"What?"

"Couldn't you have given me a buzz? You promised me an exclusive. Hang it all, I'm a newsman, first and last."

"Last, in this case," I said, smiled to myself, and felt a little better. Possibly I hadn't suffered permanent brain damage.

"You think you're bloody amusing, don't you?" said Digby in a burst of fury I wasn't prepared for. "Listen to this, Sinclair. I know bloody well why you didn't call me. You're as guilty as hell. I've got my sources. You saw Sally Ashenfelter yesterday and made damn sure she couldn't speak to anyone else. You murdered her."

"Get lost."

He ranted on. "I've written the story. It's the lead on Sunday. So you can stuff your exclusive. When I put this down, I'm going to call the police and, by Jesus, I hope they rough you up."

I slammed down the phone and went to look for the aspirin bottle. Then I moved fast.

A shower, a shave, a change of clothes. Black coffee. More black coffee.

I was using a blackthorn stick to help me around the house. Now I devoted more precious minutes to recovering my regular ebony cane, cursing Harry as I hobbled about the wet garden, hampered by the morning mist that afflicts us near the river. My shoes and trouser ends were saturated before I located the stick on the paved area in front of the summerhouse. The leather handle was soggy to the touch. I still preferred it to the blackthorn.

Back to the house. One more item to collect.

Earlier, while shaving, I'd tried to fathom Harry's behavior. Couldn't think why he'd chosen to attack me when he was already clear and on his way. I was no longer a threat. We were all but shaking hands when he'd left.

Now I understood. He'd taken the gun.

I crawled about on the living room carpet for a minute or two, feeling under furniture in case I'd kicked the thing out of sight when I staggered across the room in the night. I was wasting my time.

My brain was still functioning at ninety percent or less, but I forced it to make some deductions. Harry knew that the Colt was the murder weapon. He'd found me in possession of it. Nothing I'd said had shaken his conviction that I'd shot Morton all those years ago and was desperately covering my traces, leaving Sally to die in the burning house. The gun was his evidence. Where else could he have taken it, except to the police?

And if Harry hadn't turned me in, Digby certainly had. The squad car could be in the lane by now.

I went to the door.

The first time I tried to start the MG, it failed. What a day to let me down, the most reliable car I'd ever owned. Tried again, three or four times.

Nothing. This way I'd rapidly exhaust the battery.

Harry must have done something to immobilize the engine, blast him.

I clambered out and lifted the bonnet.

No disconnected leads that I could see. Plug covers all secure. Distributor cap in place. Everything as it should be. Not sabotage: simply the legacy of leaving the car out all night instead of garaging it. Misty weather is worse than rain for depositing a film of moisture on everything.

I collected a cloth, heated it on the kitchen boiler, and systematically dried the ignition system. Switched on again, got action first time — and overchoked. When anyone wants to make a fast getaway in the movies, they get in their cars and go. I swore, tried again, and achieved a stuttering response that persevered into a regular engine note. I was finally ready to leave.

No police car met me as I rattled up the lane. I was soon on the A4, heading west. The mist that I'd assumed was local persisted right through Marlborough, slowing my speed but making it less likely that I'd be spotted if a call had been radioed to patrol cars. It lifted for a stretch in the approach to Devizes on the A361, and as quickly returned when I was through the town.

Swiftly into Somerset. Frome, wedged steeply between two hills, where I'd disembarked from the train with my fellow evacuees in 1943. The prison town of Shepton Mallet, the stark, unhappy place where they'd based the GIs. Finally, spectrally pale in the mist, Christian Gifford.

I stopped a few hundred yards short of the farm, drove the car up a track into a wooded section where it wouldn't be seen from the lane, and walked the rest. Hard work for me, but I preferred to make my cumbersome exit from the car unobserved and out of shotgun range.

The old cliché of mist enshrouding the landscape was peculiarly apt. The absence of bird song in the country is more sepulchral than a churchyard. There was only the irregular crunch of shoes and stick on the road surface. I cursed Harry again for robbing me of my gun.

I reached the farm entrance where the milk churns waited to be collected. Ahead, in normal visibility, I would have seen the house and other buildings instead of just the blanched, overhanging hedgerow festooned with cobwebs and droplets of moisture.

I limped into the yard, my eyes compensating in mobility for my legs.

I stood for a moment scanning the gray buildings for a movement, reminded of the day when Duke and Harry had driven the jeep in there, with me in the back, triumphant, but nervous about the outcome until Barbara, radiant, her black hair springing against the white sweater, had stepped from the house and smiled.

I bit back my thoughts and approached the farmhouse.

My knock was answered by George Lockwood. Twenty years can render dramatic changes in a face. His was little altered. Some extra gaps among the teeth, a slightly more hollow look to the cheekbones, but the left eye still had its bloodshot wedge, and the eyebrows were as dark as formerly, though the rest of his hair had whitened.

He said nothing. He assessed me. The look was steady, interested, unsurprised. He knew me. He might even have expected me.

I explained superfluously, "I called on Sunday, hoping to see you and Mrs. Lockwood. I'm Theo Sinclair."

He nodded. At least I was understood.

"May I come in?"

The focus of his eyes altered. He looked past me, taking in the yard.

I told him, "I'm alone this time."

He stepped back from the door, leaving it open, and turned and shuffled along the passage.

I followed, closing the door after me.

The smell of baking wafted to me with the pungent, remembered odor of the house, the mustiness of old carpets and ancient stone. More evocative still, I heard Mrs. Lockwood's small, muted voice ask, "Who is it, George?" Then I entered the kitchen, and as she saw me she said, "Theo, my dear!" and opened her arms for me to embrace her.

She'd altered more than her husband, shed

most of the stoutness of her middle years, and acquired a network of wrinkles that gave her a depressed look when the smile receded. Arthritis had begun to deform her finger joints. She wore her hair, now silver-white, in the same severe style, scraped back from the forehead and fastened above the neck.

She said, "You can still find room for a plateful of fresh-baked scones, I reckon."

"Emphatically." More of a welcome than last time, I thought. Casually, I asked, "Where's Bernard this morning?"

"Plowing. He'll come by presently."

I tried not to register panic at the prospect. *Presently,* I remembered, has infinite limits of meaning in the West Country. You learn as much from the speaker's face as you do from the intonation. I'd never been much good at divining Mrs. Lockwood's utterances.

So the three of us sat around the old-fashioned wooden table and ate hot scones with strawberry jam and drank tea from the brown pot simmering on the range while I told them what I'd done with my life since 1944. In a few, crisp sentences.

"And what brings you back?" Mrs. Lockwood asked.

"Duke Donovan's daughter persuaded me to bring her here on Sunday. We met Bernard."

"I heard."

"Didn't have the good fortune to see you, though, so I came back."

George Lockwood now found his voice and used it expressively, on a rising note of disbelief. "Donovan had a daughter?"

"Bernard told us," Mrs. Lockwood reminded him quite sharply, adding, with a confidential smile in my direction, "Father's not so quick on the uptake as he were."

"Didn't know he were married," persisted George.

"George," said Mrs. Lockwood in a hard-pressed, discouraging voice. Turning to me, she switched to a more generous note. "Theo, my dear, have some more butter on that. 'Tisn't the war now, you know."

I took the butter dish and said, "Duke Donovan's daughter, Alice, believes her father was innocent."

"What do she know about it?" said George, not so tardy on the uptake as his wife alleged.

"She's not the only one," I said. "Do you remember Harry Ashenfelter, the other GI?"

Behind me, a new voice said, "What about Ashenfelter?" Bernard's.

I don't know how he'd managed to enter so quietly or how long he'd been there while his parents talked on, buttering their scones and registering nothing. It shook me, literally. I spilled tea on my trousers. I turned and looked into the twin barrels of the shotgun.

"Sit down, Bernard," said his mother placidly. "It's only Theo, come to see us."

"For no good purpose," said Bernard, inching

the gun towards my eyes. "He's coming with me."

Mother and son faced each other across the room, mentally squaring up. Once, I'd have backed Mrs. Lockwood. Her small voice was misleading. She possessed a steely personality with the will to enforce it, as I'd discovered painfully during the war when I learned the secondary purpose of the mangle. In those days she'd been more than a match for Bernard, large as he was. He'd always backed off. Twenty years on, I wasn't so confident. Bernard's status had altered. He was the farmer now.

To his credit, George Lockwood sided with his wife and spoke up. "What's got into 'ee today?" he demanded of Bernard. "We don't carry guns in this house."

Bernard said in a low, level voice that conceded nothing, "If the bastard do what I say, there won't be no shooting indoors." He kicked my leg hard. "Get up!"

Mrs. Lockwood scraped back her chair and slapped her gnarled right hand on the table. "Bernard, this is no way to deal with it."

"Mother," said Bernard in the same tightly controlled voice, "you'd best not interfere." This time he jabbed the muzzle of the gun hard against my throat. "Out."

The neck is a vulnerable area. There isn't much flesh to absorb such a thrust. The pain was intense, but the effect on my windpipe was worse. I hawked and gulped for breath. It was like drowning, gasping for air that couldn't reach my lungs. As I rocked forward I felt one of Bernard's hands across the breadth of my forehead, forcing it back and upward, compelling me to rise. He virtually picked me off the chair one-handedly and stood me up. I was propped against the table facing him, spluttering wretchedly.

From behind me, I heard Mrs. Lockwood repeat, more as a plea than a command, "Bernard, this isn't the way," and through my discomfort I concluded that this was the limit of her protest.

I was mistaken. She was out of her chair in the next second and round the table wrestling with him for the gun. He easily could have knocked her down, but he simply gripped the stock with one hand and the twin barrels with the other, and resisted.

They persevered with this unequal struggle for perhaps a quarter of a minute, until she gave up the attempt and settled instead for keeping a token handhold on the gun, shouting bitterly at her husband. "Can't you do nothing but sit there?"

I suspect that George Lockwood knew his son was physically more than a match for them both. He didn't stir from his seat at the table.

By now you're thinking what about Theo Sinclair? What was he doing to support the old lady and help himself? But you've got to remember the situation I was in. The shotgun was still a matter of inches from my chest. There wasn't anything I could usefully do except try to appease Bernard. I found sufficient breath to gasp, "All right, I'll go. I'm on the way out."

Bernard commented, "Too bloody true."

He'd given my words an ugly twist, turning them into a threat that I didn't seriously believe. I'd never rated him as a likely killer. He was dangerous because the shotgun was a lethal weapon, but I doubted whether he was sufficiently passionate or stupid to kill a man willfully.

So I made an appeal to his better nature. Leaning heavily on my stick, that old friend in adversity, I picked my way pathetically towards the door.

As Bernard moved the gun to keep me covered, his mother tensed again and tried to drag it downwards. There was never a chance that she could deflect the aim long enough for me to escape, but as I shortly discovered, she was more concerned about Bernard than me. She blurted out a frenzied appeal to him. "I won't let you. My son is not a killer. Thou shalt not kill. Killing is something else, Bernard."

He said tersely, "You should know, Mother," and in those four words told me what I'd come to find out.

I didn't believe it.

Mrs. Lockwood stared at him blankly. She released her grip on the gun and took a step back. She raised one hand to her mouth and pressed it edgewise between her teeth, emitting a long, stifled moan. Then she seemed to shrink into herself, crumpling into a posture of despair.

Bernard had refrained from physical aggression towards her, but his words were relentless. "Blaspheming hypocrite. Quoting the Lord's Commandments at me when the smell of death is still on you."

She'd sunk into a chair. She looked up and said, "That isn't true."

"Isn't true?" Bernard challenged her, eyes alight with the force of his recrimination. "Like yesterday?"

Mrs. Lockwood winced, as if he'd struck her. She tried to form a word and couldn't.

He aped her voice cruelly. " 'Bernard, darling, would you drive me into Frome early? I made an appointment with the optician.' Optician be buggered! I watched you go into the off-license and come out of it with two bottles of spirit in the carrier bag. I saw you make off to the railway station and buy a ticket. Your appointment weren't in Frome at all, and it weren't with no optician. You took the train to Bath." He half turned and said, "Father! Have you looked at the paper, seen what happened to Sally Ashenfelter yesterday?"

Old George Lockwood had emerged enough from his passive state to stare in horror at his wife.

Bernard continued inexorably to nail the charge. "Mother were always claiming to be sorry for Sally and her weakness for liquor. Forever meaning to visit her again for old time's sake. Well, she finally did, with two bottles of vodka and a box of matches."

Then George spoke up with surprising tenderness. "Molly, what have you done, my love? You promised no more killing. No more blood, you said."

There was a pained cry from Mrs. Lockwood. "I did it to protect us. It was all forgotten and then —" She covered her face.

Bernard was unmoved. He tightened his grip on the gun and gestured to me to get out.

I was reeling under a welter of emotions, repelled, shocked, angry, and pitying. I might as well own up to a slight sense of gratification too. My assumption that the answer to the mystery lay here, with the Lockwoods, had been right. But I hadn't cast Mrs. Lockwood as a double murderess.

Had you?

Do you need any more convincing?

I did. I backtracked mentally to 1943 and spun the crucial events at the speed of a tape recorder on fast forward. Morton having Barbara in the barn. Me, blurting out my story. To Duke. And to Mrs. Lockwood.

Duke didn't murder Morton. He looked into the barn, listened, reached his own conclusion, and left.

The Lockwoods had put a ban on Morton. Incensed, Mrs. Lockwood collected the gun from the hallstand drawer. To her, it was irrelevant whether Morton had just raped her daughter or made love to her. She shot him at point-blank range, dropped the gun, and brought Barbara back to the farmhouse.

Sally and I had been in the farmhouse kitchen when Mrs. Lockwood brought Barbara in. Sally, and only Sally outside the family, knew that Barbara and Morton were lovers and that Barbara's hysteria couldn't have been caused by rape.

Yet when Duke was put on trial, Sally wasn't called as a witness. Mine was the evidence that had hanged Duke. Mine, and the Lockwoods'. Prosecution and defense both accepted that Morton was killed because he attacked Barbara. Sally's story conflicted with both.

They gossiped about poor Sally's alcoholism in Christian Gifford, but only one couple knew the reason for it: the Lockwoods. So when Alice and I turned up at Gifford Farm and learned from Bernard that Sally was living in Bath, Mrs. Lockwood saw disaster looming. She made an appointment with Sally and bought some vodka.

A murder cold-bloodedly planned and executed.

And not the last I have to describe.

If you're of a nervous disposition or hoping to get some peaceful sleep in the next hours, better close the book at this point. Thanks for your company, and good night.

For you, the unshakably persistent page-turner, I'll tell the rest as it happened. We left Bernard pointing the shotgun at me, maneuvering me out of the farmhouse. His mother was sobbing her guilty heart out while the hapless George attempted to comfort her.

I cooperated by opening the door and stepping into the yard. I suppose it was too optimistic to hope that Bernard would let me make a discreet exit while he sorted out his domestic crisis. He prodded me in the back with the shotgun to let me know he was right behind me.

Try to take the heat out of this, I thought. I told him as casually as I could, "I left my car up the lane, but there's no need for you to come with me."

Bernard ignored me. He said in a toneless statement of fact that was more chilling than a threat, "You're going across to the barn."

I said, "What for?"

He answered in the same level tone. "You've got to be put down."

Like a stricken animal.

My first reaction was petrified funk. A few seconds of numbness, when I felt as if my feet weren't in contact with the ground. Then anger. The urge to lash out and fight for my life.

I didn't stand a chance.

Reason, I told myself. *You've got some wits. Use them.*

I said, "That's murder you're talking about."

He stuck the gun harder into my backbone, forcing me forward. I limped slowly towards the barn, the same small barn where Morton had been shot. The stone building set back from the rest, its gray-tiled roof hoary from the freezing mist.

Talk to him. It's all you can do.

"You don't want to kill me," I told him, putting it as a genial observation between friends. "That's sure to make more trouble for you. You're not a murderer, Bernard. You don't have to repeat your mother's mistakes."

He muttered behind me, "Step out or I'll drop you here."

I kept moving, talking as we went, trying desperately to hammer home the message. "You've got no blood on your hands. It was your father who helped her dispose of Morton's body after she shot him, wasn't it? He put the head in one of his cider barrels and buried the rest somewhere off the farm. He meant to keep the barrel here, but someone mistakenly loaded it onto a lorry and delivered it to the Shorn Ram. That's what happened, isn't it?"

We were twenty yards from the barn door, and for all the response I'd got, I could have saved my breath. I was going to need it.

I persisted, "Your father's an accessory after the fact, but you're in the clear. There's no way you can cover up your parents' crimes. The police are coming here. The press. *News on Sunday* is sending a man. Today, Bernard. They're on their way."

We reached the barn. I thought about dashing inside and slamming the door in his face, but for me, it could only be a thought. It assumed agility that I didn't possess.

Nor was my stick any use as a weapon against a shotgun jammed into my kidneys. He'd pull the trigger before I raised my arm. I knew he wasn't bluffing. There's an instinct, a primitive, feral sense that operates when death is imminent.

A bead of sweat ran down my side, as if it were high summer.

I went in.

The barn was moderately dark but not dark enough for me to surprise him with a sudden dive out of range.

What could I do, short of begging for my life?

I said, "It's your future as well as mine. Have you thought of that?"

Bernard dug the muzzle harder into my back. "Up there." He wanted me to climb up to the hayloft where the previous murder had been committed. The precise place. The sweat on my body turned to ice. I'd assumed up to now that I was addressing a man who was rational, if hostile. At this moment I lost that confidence. He was planning a ritual slaughter.

Standing by the ladder to the hayloft, I told him flatly, "I can't climb this."

Immediately I keeled off-balance. He'd kicked my stick clean out of my hand. Instinctively, I grabbed one of the rungs of the ladder to stop myself falling. I hit the wood as I swung around it.

A piercing pain hit the small of my back, as if one of my ribs had snapped. Then another. He was jabbing me viciously in the kidneys with the point of the gun.

I groped upwards and started climbing like a demented ape to pull myself clear. Using my arms alone, I hauled myself most of the way, then got some leverage with my good leg and forced my aching body high enough to get a hold on the joist supporting the ladder. I put out a knee and heaved myself onto the boards.

Up there I doubled and writhed in agony as the pain bit into my back. I don't think I cared if he put a shot through my head, so long as he didn't attack my kidneys again. I rolled against the nearest bale of straw to protect them. But as the spasms subsided to tolerable levels and I became more conscious of my surroundings, I realized that Bernard hadn't followed me up the ladder. I heard it scrape against the joist and hit the floor with a thud. For some unfathomable reason he'd pulled it away from the hayloft and stranded me up there.

There comes a stage when acute pain turns to a throbbing, generalized ache. I reached out for a handhold and dragged my protesting body close enough to give me a view over the edge. Then I forced myself to watch what was happening below me. I couldn't believe that Bernard would simply leave me stranded in the hayloft. He meant to kill me, and I was damn sure nothing I'd said had shaken his resolution.

He'd rested the shotgun against the wall. For some obscure reason, he was rearranging the bales, dragging one from the back of the barn towards the center, then a second one. He took a knife from his pocket, cut the cord on the second bale, and scattered loose hay across the floor.

Presently he disappeared from view below me, and I heard a muffled, dragging sound, which I assumed was a third bale about to be added to the stack.

I was wrong. The object that Bernard was tugging across the barn was a body. A dead body. Male.

The jacket and shirt were heavily blood-stained. I couldn't tell yet if I knew the face, because it was upside down from my vantage point.

Irrespective of who it was, I shivered. I understood now why Bernard had shrugged off my warnings. It was no use telling him that killing me would be something else, a different class of crime, because he'd already enrolled himself for the class. He was blooded, a killer like his mother.

Reasoning with him was a futile exercise. He meant to kill me, too, and there was no way I could dissuade him.

I watched him hump the corpse onto the bales. They served as a catafalque, as if for a lying-in-state. Except that the body was spread-eagled across the top with legs apart, one arm hanging down and eyes open, seeming to stare up at me.

I stared back, for the face was right-way-up now, and I could see who it was.

Harry Ashenfelter.

TWENTY-TWO

Death had colored him blue and white. A leaden blue with blotches of white down the left side of the forehead, cheekbone, and jaw. He'd been face down on a hard surface for some time, and these were the points of contact. I didn't have to be a pathologist to work that out. Another observation for the medics among you: his limbs had flopped over the sides of the bales, so rigor mortis had not yet developed to any obvious extent. As I picture the scene, it helps me to be clinical. It subdues the horror.

I stared down at him from the loft with more respect than I'd felt for him as a living being. He'd shown precious little concern for either of his wives while they were alive, but it seemed that some vestige of loyalty or husbandly duty towards Sally had impelled him to try to find her murderer. He must have driven through the night to Somerset after leaving me stunned in Pangbourne. He'd believed me when I'd told him that the answer to the mystery would be found at Gifford Farm. Like me, he'd decided to investigate alone.

For this, he'd been shot through the heart.

These people were steeped in blood.

My turn next.

You, my wily reader, may already have deduced how Bernard Lockwood proposed to kill me. I hadn't. I must tell you that my blitzed brain was barely functioning. I couldn't think past the shock of Harry's corpse.

My eyes were still on him when I heard the creak of the barn door. Bernard had opened it and stepped outside.

I blinked, snapped my thoughts roughly together, and shifted my focus. He'd taken the shotgun with him.

Escape, an inner voice urgently told me. *Move yourself. Get out of here. You can break your fall on the bales. All right, there's a body down there, but he's dead, and that's how you'll be if you're squeamish now.*

I braced myself. Felt a paralyzing pain in my back as I heaved myself up into a crouching position. Looked down into Harry's sightless eyes. Froze.

The door creaked a second time, and Bernard came in again, without the shotgun. He was carrying something just as lethal: a can of petrol.

Without even raising his eyes, he unscrewed the cap and literally doused Harry's body and the bales it was mounted on. The fumes wafted up to me. It wasn't a catafalque that I was looking down on. It was a funeral pyre. It would dispose of Harry as soon as it was lit. Not to mention me, trapped ten feet above him.

I shouted, "Bloody maniac!"

Oblivious, Bernard busied himself on the flag-stone floor, drawing loose hay by the armful into a narrow, heaped trail leading from the body towards the door. As he backed away from me I yelled more abuse at him. To no effect.

He didn't lay the trail all the way to the door. About six feet short, he stopped. He wanted space to turn and get out quickly. He pushed open the door.

Next he went methodically back along the line of hay, sprinkling it with petrol, priming the fuse he'd created. Then he returned to the door, set the can on the floor, felt in his pocket, and produced a cigarette lighter.

He flicked his thumb to light the thing. I saw it spark, but no flame appeared. At the second try the fuel ignited and was immediately blown out by a draft from the doorway. It was straight out of Hitchcock when I think about it. Everything set for a mighty burn-up, and the lighter refuses to function. He shielded it against his chest with his free hand and tried again.

This time the flame sprouted. Bernard squatted and tentatively extended the lighter towards the fuse of petrol-soaked hay.

Then, amazingly, a figure appeared through the door, holding the shotgun.

For pity's sake, I can practically hear you say. Not the old cliché of the man who appears in the door with a gun. Spare us that!

Well, for a start, it wasn't a man. It was a girl.

And she was holding the gun by the wrong end, like a sledgehammer. At that moment I sincerely blessed Alice Ashenfelter. I forgave her all the hassle, the slanderous things she'd accused me of, the brazen intrusions into my life and work. This was one intrusion that I welcomed unreservedly.

She gripped the muzzle and crashed the thick wooden stock onto Bernard's crouching form. A bold swipe that had to be right the first time.

Unhappily it wasn't.

Bernard must have glimpsed the movement at the edge of his vision, because he ducked suddenly, dipping his head and swaying away. The gun caught his right shoulder, merely toppling him off-balance. Alice gave a frustrated cry and sheered aside, dropping the gun with a clatter.

Bernard wasn't hurt. He made a diving tackle and brought Alice down like a skittle. She kicked out and managed to wiggle clear on all fours.

He picked himself up without hurrying and stalked her, out of my line of sight, to the interior of the barn below the hayloft. She was trapped.

I heard her scream, "Theo!"

I threw myself over the edge.

Up to now life had spared me from the sight of a dead person, let alone a physical contact. The prospect repelled me. Yet this was a reaction so automatic and instantaneous that I was unaffected. I dropped onto Harry's lifeless form, felt the flesh under the clothes respond flaccidly to my weight, touched one of the cold hands and saw it flop aside, then dragged myself clear and down to floor level.

My eyes were on Bernard. He was ten feet away from me, in a semi-crouch, with Alice flat to the floor beside him. I would have said face down, were it not that her face was up, and stressfully so. Bernard was grasping the root of her plait, tugging at her head, while his knee pinned her chest to the floor. Her neck looked ready to snap any second.

She gave an agonized moan.

I'd started a rescue act I wasn't equipped to complete. With my stick way out of reach on the other side of the barn, the best I could hope to do was crawl towards them, and then Bernard would tear me to pieces and have me on toast.

There had to be a better way.

The previous night, Harry had taken the Colt .45 from my house. If he still had it . . .

I put my hand up to the corpse and pressed it against the jacket pocket.

Nothing.

The other pocket, then.

Couldn't reach.

Another cry of pain from Alice.

I grabbed the body with both hands and tugged it towards me, off the bales. It toppled heavily onto me. Next second, I was wrestling with a dead man.

Thank God my arms are strong. I pushed him

upwards and to one side and sat up in the same movement.

Alice gave a more piercing scream.

I felt for Harry's right-hand pocket and this time located the gun. I tugged it out, leveled it at Bernard, and squeezed the trigger.

The bullet ripped into his back. He was thrown forward, face first, collapsing across a bale of hay. I don't know if he was dead, but I didn't fire a second shot.

Alice lay still for a second, gasping, then rolled over and looked towards me, wide-eyed in horror.

"You're on fire!"

I wasn't — much. Harry was. His saturated clothes were ablaze. I'm not sure if it was Bernard's lighter or the gunshot that had ignited the petrol. I jerked away from the corpse and ripped off my smoldering jacket.

The speed of a petrol fire is awesome. I looked towards the door and saw huge white-and-yellow flames leaping for the gap. We'd never get out through there.

Alice was on her feet and beside me, trying to drag me to the other side of the barn where the fire wasn't raging yet. With her help I crawled and slithered across, but there wasn't much comfort there. No petrol, certainly, but black smoke swirled in our faces. They say that you usually suffocate before you burn.

"The ladder," I shouted, dragging myself upright against a beam. If we could get up there, the hayloft would screen us from the worst of the flames and the heat. I wasn't thinking about survival, just the immediate need to put something between us and the fire.

Together we hoisted the ladder and propped it against the hayloft. The heat was intense. There was a roar like Niagara, and things were cracking and spitting all round us.

Alice shinnied up first.

You may think this ridiculous, but I looked for my stick before I followed her. I groped in the hay until I found it and threw it up. Then I grabbed the ladder and climbed rapidly hand over hand, with a technique that was improving with practice.

Up there, the smoke was the main problem. Alice had unfurled her polo-neck collar to cover her mouth.

I'll take some credit now for smart thinking. I gestured to her to help me pull up the ladder.

Together we hauled it up to our level. It was blackened and smoking at the lower end. I indicated to Alice that we should use it as a battering ram to attack the tiled roof from the underside.

It was a high risk. There was a chance that the flames would be drawn up and leap through any gap we made. I pinned my faith on the loft floor screening us for long enough to make an escape. At the rate the fire was progressing, the floor couldn't last many minutes more. It was a moot point whether it would collapse from underneath before the sparks ignited the bales stored on top.

I propped myself on a bale, and with Alice guiding the front of the ladder, we drew it back and thrust it against the tiles at the innermost end of the loft. All we got was a numbing jolt in our arms. I thought cynically of the truism that old structures like this were built to last. Oh, for a nineteenth-century jerry-builder or an apprentice tiler on his first job.

We gave it another crack. With an exhilarating crunch, two tiles split open together and the end of the ladder projected through. We tugged it back and drove at the rest more frenziedly. Another tile fell out, and then, praise be, a group of four. A sizable hole. We dropped the ladder and rushed forward, desperate for air. I picked up my stick and poked out more tiles, then signaled to Alice to climb through.

She was quick. I tried pushing the ladder through after her, thinking we could use it to get down from the roof, but she shouted, "Theo, forget it. It's too short!"

I could feel the heat of the loft floor through my shoes. I told Alice to move aside. Then I hauled up a bale of hay and thrust it through the gap and over the edge of the building. It would cushion our landing when we jumped. I dragged another towards me and shoved it after the first.

Alice cried, "Theo, for God's sake!"

I climbed out onto the tiles.

The top couldn't have been much over fifteen

feet, and the smoke gushing out behind us was a strong incentive to jump. I looked down at the bales and said a familiar phrase. "All right, then?"

Alice was black-faced, and her glasses were peppered with carbon. She smiled and put out her hand to me and we jumped together.

TWENTY-THREE

"I hope to God I had the exposure right," said Digby for the third time at least. "If you'd given me more warning, I'd have brought a photographer with me."

"Quit complaining, will you?" Alice told him in an uprush of anger, letting the tension out. "You got your scoop."

Digby bunched his shoulders and tried to look uninvolved, like a perching vulture.

"What's one picture?" demanded Alice.

In a pained voice Digby said, "You two jumping off the blazing roof? I'll tell you what it is. It's 'Escape From Death Barn' — the shot of a lifetime. Millions will see it on the front page of their paper tomorrow."

Tomorrow. I didn't want to know about tomorrow. Coping with the past was more than I could manage. The three of us were sitting around the kitchen table in the farmhouse. One young constable was in attendance. In another room, Inspector Voss was questioning the Lockwoods. Across the yard, a fire crew was hosing the gutted barn.

"Let me get this right," I said to Digby, letting

my resentment show. "You were actually waiting outside with a camera while Alice and I were in that inferno in danger of our lives?"

"It's not a pressman's job to get involved, old man."

"Oh, for Christ's sake, Digby."

"I couldn't have got near, anyway, once the fire started."

"Before it started, you stood and watched Alice go in there to tackle a man of Bernard Lockwood's size?"

Digby said blandly, "She acted independently, didn't you, my dear?"

Alice ignored him and said to me. "What happened is this, Theo. I read in the paper about Sally being killed in the fire, and I knew I was wrong about you — shooting Morton, I mean. Whoever killed Sally did it to silence her. They were scared of you and me getting to speak to her. Whatever mean and hostile things I said about you, you're no cold-blooded killer. I thought of Harry first, but I couldn't see him burning his own house, and I was certain he wouldn't actively harm Sally, for all his insensitivity. I mean, he was willing to let her speak to us on Sunday. He was really upset when she got drunk. So who else could have done it? The answer had to be at Gifford Farm. After Digby called you on the phone and you hung up on him, I told him that's where we have to go. He snatched up a camera and drove us here fast. We left the car up the lane and came in quietly to avoid Bernard and his shotgun, if we could."

"We saw the kitchen door open," put in Digby, "so I advised a discreet withdrawal to the farm-machinery shed."

"Then we saw you come out of the back door with Bernard holding his gun to your back."

"And what did you make of that?" I asked Alice with faint amusement. "Me — your number-one suspect."

I believe Alice reddened under the smears of soot. "I already told you, I changed my mind about that. Anyway, Bernard took you into the barn. After a while he came out and put down the shotgun and collected the gasoline, so I went closer and took a peek inside. When I saw him pouring gas over the floor, I thought, Somebody's got to stop this." She sighed and gave a weary smile. "I could use a few lessons in how to disable a man."

I reached out my hand and clasped it over hers. "You did all right. I'd never have got out alive without you."

At this she laughed suddenly and openly. "I figure you'd never have been *in* there if you hadn't met me."

I think it was the first time I'd seen her laugh without a trace of unease or suspicion in her features. Her glasses were twisted askew and her elegant nose was heavily smudged, but I warmed to her. I laughed too. Then I said impulsively, "Now that we've straightened out a few things, let's meet again."

Digby felt into his pocket and said, "I'll quote that, if you don't mind."

I said, "Shut up."

But as you, my loyal reader, will appreciate, life isn't what you want, it's what you get. Alice had her return flight booked for the following day. We didn't even manage a night out together, or a night in, because that puddinghead Voss kept me waiting for the rest of the afternoon and evening sorting out what had happened in the barn. I admitted to shooting Bernard in self-defense, which seem straightforward enough, but Voss tied himself in knots trying to decide whether it was manslaughter or justifiable homicide. As they didn't propose to charge me, anyway, I lost all patience with them. By the time I was free to leave, Digby had long since driven Alice back to Reading.

Digby's photograph didn't turn out, by the way, but he still had his exclusive story, and I'm sure he was well paid for it.

If you're looking for an upbeat ending, there's not much I can offer. George Lockwood admitted to his part in disposing of Morton's body in 1943. He took the police to a lake near Frome where he'd weighted and sunk the headless corpse. They sent some frogmen down, but after so long, it wasn't surprising that nothing was found.

Mrs. Molly Lockwood was convicted of the murder of Sally Ashenfelter and was given a life sentence. She also confessed to shooting Clifford Morton in 1943 and to perjury at the trial of Duke Donovan. In view of her advanced age, the Director of Public Prosecutions deferred bringing her to court on these charges.

The Home Secretary recommended a posthumous Royal Pardon for Duke, which I know pleased Alice. It pleased me.

People have been telling me for years not to blame myself for my part in Duke's conviction. They say I couldn't have done any different, that I spoke what I understood to be the truth. Right. But I can't forget. I never will.

I promised you an extraordinary story, and I've done my best to deliver it. One more development may be of interest. In 1965, I applied for a visiting lectureship to Yale University, and to my delight and good fortune I was taken on. Yale is only twenty-five miles south of Waterbury, Connecticut.

At the time I told myself I must be out of my mind. On occasions I still say that I was, and then Alice laughs and pours me another drink.

Of lager, from a can.